DOCTOR DOLITTLE
AND
THE GREEN CANARY

THE YEARLING DOCTOR DOLITTLE BOOKS

DOCTOR DOLITTLE

AND THE
GREEN CANARY

WRITTEN AND ILLUSTRATED BY
HUGH LOFTING

THE CENTENARY EDITION
A YEARLING BOOK

Published by
Dell Publishing
a division of
The Bantam Doubleday Dell Publishing Group, Inc.
666 Fifth Avenue
New York, New York 10103

ISBN: 0-440-40079-1

Printed in the United States of America

September 1988

10 9 8 7 6 5 4 3 2 1

CW

I would like to acknowledge the following editors, whose faith in the literary value of these children's classics was invaluable in the publication of the new editions: Janet Chenery, consulting editor; Olga Fricker, Hugh Lofting's sister-in-law, who worked closely with the author and edited the last four original books; Lori Mack, associate editor at Dell; and Lois Myller, whose special love for Doctor Dolittle helped make this project possible.

CHRISTOPHER LOFTING

· Introduction ·

WHEN my husband, Hugh Lofting, wrote and illustrated the story of Pippinella, the green canary, for the *Herald Tribune* Syndicate, his intention was to publish it one day in book form. He used some of the material in *Doctor Dolittle's Caravan*, in which the little canary appeared as the prima donna of the Doctor's canary opera and became a well-loved and established member of the Doctor's household. However, Mr. Lofting found so much of Pippinella's story still untold in book form that he began organizing another volume to include all the exciting adventures that had befallen the Doctor's little friend before she joined the caravan, as well as those she experienced with Doctor Dolittle after the canary opera was over.

It was never quite finished. But so near had Mr. Lofting come to doing so that I felt I must find a way to do it for him. When my sister, Olga Michael, whose desire to write had been applauded and encouraged by my husband, and who had given him much help during the compiling of the new material for Pippinella, offered to finish it, I was delighted.

And so, here it is: the completed story of the green

canary, all written by Hugh Lofting with the exception of a brief first chapter to introduce the Doctor and his family to new readers and a dramatic and exciting concluding chapter to round out the life of the unusual little bird, Pippinella. I truly believe my husband would have approved.

JOSEPHINE LOFTING

· Contents ·

· Illustrations ·

PART ONE

· The First Chapter ·

THE DOCTOR MEETS
THE GREEN CANARY

HIS story of the further adventures of Pippinella, the green canary, begins during the time of the Dolittle Circus. It will tell—in much greater detail—the strange events that took place in the life of the little bird before she came to live with John Dolittle. Pippinella was a rare kind of canary that the Doctor had found in an animal shop while taking a walk with Matthew Mugg, the cat's-meat man. Thinking he had made a bad bargain because—as he thought—hen canaries couldn't sing, he had been greatly astonished to find she had a most unusual mezzo-contralto voice.

And what was more unusual still, she had traveled many thousands of miles and lived a most varied and interesting life. When she had told the Doctor some of the dramatic happenings that led up to her being sold to the animal shop he interrupted her.

"You know, Pippinella," he said, "for many years now, I have wanted to do a series of animal biographies. But because most birds and animals have such poor memories for details, I have never been able to get onto paper a complete record of any one animal. However, you seem to have the knack for remembering the proper things. You're a born storyteller. Would you be willing to help me write your biography?"

"Why, certainly, Doctor," replied Pippinella. "When would you like to begin?"

"Any time you feel rested enough," said the Doctor. "I'll have Too-Too fetch me some extra notebooks from the storage tent. How about tomorrow evening after the circus is closed up for the night?"

"All right," said the canary. "I'll be happy to begin tomorrow. I *am* sort of tired tonight."

This conversation, which the Doctor had with the green canary, was all carried on in the bird's own language. John Dolittle had learned, many years before, to speak the language of animals and birds. This unique ability had earned for him the friendship and loyalty of all living creatures and had influenced him to change his doctoring of humans to a busy life of caring for the illnesses and injuries of animals.

While the Doctor was talking with Pippinella about writing her biography, the members of his household had withdrawn to a corner of the wagon and were carrying on a lively discussion. Gub-Gub the pig, Dab-Dab the duck, Jip the dog, and Too-Too the owl were quite indignant that the Doctor should choose a newcomer to the group for this great honor. Whitey the white mouse, being more timid than the others, just listened and thought about the idea. But Gub-Gub, the most conceited of the lot, said that he was going to speak to the Doctor about it.

So the next evening, when the family had gathered in the wagon to hear the continuation of the canary's story, Gub-Gub cleared his throat nervously and spoke up.

"I don't see why anyone would want to read the biography of a mere canary," he grumbled. "My life is much more interesting. Why, the places I've been! Africa, Asia, and the Fiji Islands. Not to mention the food I've eaten. I'm a celebrity for that if for nothing else. Now, what can a canary know about food—eating nothing but dried-up seeds and bread crumbs? And where could she go—cooped up in a cage most of her life?"

"Food! Food! That's all you think about," snapped Too-Too. "I think it's more important to be a good mathematician. Take me, for instance: I know to the penny how much gold there is in the Bank of England!"

"I have a gold collar from a king," said Jip. "That's something!"

"I suppose it's nothing that I can make a bed so it's fit for decent folk to sleep in!" snapped Dab-Dab. "And who, I'd like to know, keeps you all healthy and well fed. I think that's more important!"

Whitey just sat there and didn't say a word; he didn't really think his life was interesting enough for a biography. When the Doctor looked at him with a questioning expression on his face, Whitey dropped his eyelids and pretended to be asleep.

"Haven't *you* anything to say, Whitey?" asked the Doctor.

"No, sir—I mean, yes!" said the white mouse timidly. "I think the biography of Pippinella will be very nice."

"Well, let's get on with it, then," said the Doctor. "Please —if you're ready—we are, Pippinella."

The canary then told them how she had been born in an aviary—a small one where the man who raised canaries gave her special attention because of her unusual voice; how she came to be such a rare shade of green because her father was a lemon-yellow Harz Mountain canary and her mother a greenfinch of very good family; and how she had shared a nest with three brothers and two sisters—until it

HUGH LOFTING

" 'I think it's more important to be a good mathematician,'
snapped Too-Too"

was discovered that she was that rare thing: a hen bird
who sang as beautifully as a cock.

Pippinella explained that it wasn't true that hens
couldn't sing as well as cocks. It was only that cocks didn't
encourage their womenfolk to sing, saying that a woman's
job was to care for the young and to make a home for her
husband and children.

Because of her beautiful voice Pippinella acquired a

master who bought her and carried her off to a new home, an inn where travelers from all over the world stopped on their way to the seaport to eat and sleep the night.

After the canary had described the inn more fully the Doctor interrupted her to ask, "Pardon me, Pippinella. Could that have been the inn on the road from London to Liverpool? I believe it is called the Inn of the Seven Seas."

"That's the one, Doctor," answered the little bird. "Have you been there?"

"Indeed we have," replied John Dolittle, "several times."

Gub-Gub jumped up so suddenly from his chair that he crashed into the table where Pippinella sat telling her story and sent the water out of the canary's drinking dish sloshing over the sides.

"I remember!" he cried. "That's where the turnips were especially good—done with a parsley sauce and a little dash of nutmeg."

"If I'm not mistaken," said Jip, "I left a perfectly good knucklebone buried there. Cook gave it to me right after dinner and I planned to eat it later. But the Doctor was in such a hurry to move on, I hadn't a moment to dig it up before we left."

"I'll bet you wished many times that you had it, eh, Jip?" said Too-Too. "But then, you must have had plenty of bones buried back at Puddleby."

"Not more than three or four," Jip replied. "Those were lean days."

"They would have been leaner if I'd not found that gold sovereign just as we were leaving," piped up Whitey.

"Gold sovereign?" asked the Doctor. "You didn't tell me about it. Whatever did you do with it, Whitey?"

Whitey looked confused and kept glancing from Dab-Dab back to the Doctor. He wished he'd kept quiet about the sovereign.

Dab-Dab ruffled her feathers and made a clucking noise.

"He gave it to me, John Dolittle!" she said crossly. "How do you think we would have eaten at all after that scoundrel Blossom departed with all the circus funds? You know our larder was empty, Doctor. Except for about a teaspoonful of tea and some moldy tapioca."

"But the sovereign didn't belong to you," said the Doctor.

"It did—just as much as to anyone else," said Whitey. "It was lying in the dust right smack between the hind feet of one of the coach horses. And he was trampling and kicking up the dirt so that I could hardly keep my eyes on it—good as they are."

"No one but Whitey—with his microscopic eyes—would ever have seen it," said Dab-Dab. "There was no point in running around asking stableboys and kitchen maids if it belonged to them. Who could recognize a gold sovereign as his? Anyway, it's spent now—that was almost a year ago."

"Well, well," sighed the Doctor. "I suppose it was all right. Shall we get on with the story, Pippinella?"

"I was treated with great respect and admiration by the owner of the inn and his wife and children," continued the canary. "And I made many friends there. Everybody stopped to speak to me and listen to my songs—it was very gratifying.

"On nice days my master would hang my cage on a hook high up beside the entrance to the inn. There I would greet the incoming guests with my very best songs. One little verse I made up and set to music became very popular with everyone who heard it. I called it 'Maids, Come Out; the Coach Is Here,' and whenever I heard the sound of approaching horses, I'd sing it at the top of my lungs to announce to the stableboys and porters that another coachload of travelers was nearing the inn.

"Among the people who came to be my friends was one named Jack, who drove the night coach from the north. For him I composed a merry tune called 'The Harness Jingle.' Old Jack would call out to me, as he rolled his coach into the noisy courtyard, 'Hulloa, there, Pip! Hulloa!' and I'd answer him by singing another verse of his song."

· The Second Chapter ·
THE INN OF THE SEVEN SEAS

AFTER a short pause the green canary continued her story.

"Besides the many friends that I made among the people in that place I made lots more among the animals. I knew all the coach horses and I would hail them by name as they came trotting into the yard. And I had dog friends too: the watchdog who lived in a kennel by the gate and several terriers who hung about the stables. They knew all the local gossip of the town. There was a dovecote above the loft where they kept the hay for the horses. And here carrier pigeons lived who were trained to fly long distances with messages. And many were the interesting tales that they could tell of an evening, when they sat on the gutters of the roof or strutted about the yard beneath my cage, picking up the bits of corn that had fallen from the horses' feed bags.

"Yes, as I look back over all the places I have been, that nice, busy old inn seems as good a home as any cage bird could wish to find.

"I had been there, I suppose, about five months when, just as the poplars were beginning to turn yellow, I noticed a peculiar thing: knots of people used to gather in the yard of an evening and talk with serious, worried faces. I listened to such conversations as were near enough for me to hear. But although I knew by this time the meaning of a great number of human words I couldn't make anything out of this talk. It seemed to be mostly about what you call politics. There was an air of restlessness. Everybody seemed to be expecting or fearing something.

"And then one day, for the first time, I saw soldiers. They came tramping into the inn yard in the morning. They had heavy packs on their backs. Evidently they had been marching all night because many of them were so weary that they sat down against the stable wall with their boots covered with dust and slept. They stayed with us till the following day, eating their meals in the yard, out of little tin dishes that they took from the packs they had carried.

"Some of them had friends among the maids of the inn. And when they left I noticed that two of the maids who waved to them from the dining-room window were weeping. There was quite a crowd to see them go off. And very smart they looked in their red coats, marching out of the gate in rows of four with their guns on their shoulders and their packs on their backs, stepping in time to the drummer's *rap-rap, rappatap, tap, tap!*

"Not many days after they had gone we had another new kind of excitement, another army. But this one did not wear smart uniforms or march to the beat of a drum. It was composed of ragged people, wild-eyed, untidy, and disorderly! They came scrambling into the inn yard, shouting and waving sticks. A leader among them stood on an upturned bucket and made them a speech. The owner of the inn begged the leader to take them away. He was evidently very worried about having them in his yard. But the leader wouldn't listen. When one speech was finished

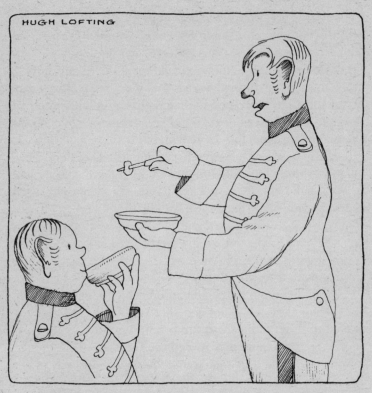

HUGH LOFTING

"Eating their meals in the yard, out of little tin dishes"

another would begin. But what any of them was about I couldn't make out.

"Finally the ragged mob drifted away of its own accord. And as soon as the yard was clear the innkeeper shut and locked the gate so they couldn't come back.

"I asked one of my pigeon friends what it all meant. He shook his head seriously, 'I don't quite know,' he said. 'Something's been going on for weeks now. I hope it isn't war. Two of the carriers, the best flyers in the dovecote, were taken away last Monday. We don't know where they went to. But those two pigeons were used for carrying war messages before.'

" 'What is war?' I asked.

" 'Oh, it's a messy, stupid business,' he said. 'Two sides wave flags and beat drums and shoot one another dead. It always begins this way, making speeches, talking about rights, and all that sort of thing.'

" 'But what is it for? What do they get out of it?'

" 'I don't know,' he said. 'To tell you the truth, I don't think they know themselves. When I was young I carried war messages myself once. But it never seemed to me that anyone, not even the generals, knew any more of what it was all about than I did.' "

Pippinella stopped in her story long enough to take a sip of water and then went on again.

"That same week that the ragged people came to the inn to make speeches, we had still another unusual arrival. This was a frightfully elegant private coach. It had a wonderful picture painted on the door, handles and mountings of silver, outriders on fine horses, to guard it, and altogether it was the grandest equipage I had ever seen.

"On its first appearance way down the road I had started singing my usual song, 'Maids, Come Out,' and so forth. And I was still singing when it came to a halt in the yard and a tall, superior sort of gentleman got out of it. The innkeeper was already on the steps, bowing low, and porters were standing around to help the guest out and to attend to his luggage. But strangely enough, the first thing that the elegant person took any notice of was myself.

" 'By Jove!' he said, putting a quizzing glass to his eye and sauntering toward my cage. 'What a marvelous singer! Is it a canary?'

" 'Yes, my lord,' said the host, coming forward, 'a green canary.'

" 'I'll buy it from you,' said the elegant gentleman. 'Buckley, my secretary, will pay you whatever the price is. Have it ready to travel with me in the morning, please.'

"I saw the innkeeper's face fall at this. For he was very much attached to me and the idea of selling me, even for a big price, evidently did not appeal to him. But this grand person was clearly someone who he was afraid to displease by refusing.

" 'Very good, my lord,' said he in a low voice, and he followed the guest into the hotel.

"For my part I was greatly disturbed. Life here was very pleasant. I did not wish to exchange it for something I knew nothing of. However, I had been sold. There was nothing I could do about it. That is perhaps the biggest disadvantage in being a cage bird: you're not allowed to choose your own owner or home.

"Well, after they had gone inside the inn I was sitting on my perch pondering rather miserably over this new turn of affairs, when along came my chaffinch friend who nested in the yard.

" 'Listen,' I said. 'Who is this haughty person who drove up in the coach just now?'

" 'Oh, that's the Marquis,' said he. 'A very big swell. He owns half the country around here—mills, mines, farms, and everything. He's frightfully rich and powerful. Why do you ask?'

" 'He has bought me,' I said. 'Just told the innkeeper to wrap me up—like a pound of cheese or something—without even asking first if he wanted to sell me.'

" 'Yes,' said the chaffinch, nodding his head, 'the Marquis is like that. He takes it for granted that everybody will do what he wants—and most people do, for that matter. He's awfully powerful. However, there are some who think things are going to change. That meeting, you remember, when the workmen and ragged people came here making speeches? Well, that was mostly over him. He has put a whole lot of machinery into the mills and mines, it seems. There has been a terrible lot of grumbling and bad feeling over it. It is even whispered that the Marquis's life is in danger all the time now.'

" 'Well,' I said, 'he won't get me to do what he wants. If he takes me away from here, I won't sing another note. So there!'

" 'I don't see why you should grumble,' he said. 'You will have the most elegant home. Why, he lives in a castle with more than a hundred servants, they say. I know he has a tremendous lot of gardeners myself because I've built my nest in his garden, and I've seen them. If you ask me, I should say you're very lucky.'

" 'I don't care anything about his hundred servants,' I said. 'I don't like his face. I want to live here with the host and his family and old Jack and the other coach drivers. They are my friends. If the Marquis takes me away, I'll stop singing.'

" 'That's rather a joke,' chuckled the chaffinch thoughtfully. 'The all-powerful Marquis getting defied by a cage bird. He got his way with everybody till he met a canary who didn't like his face! Splendid! I must go to tell that to the wife.'

"Well, the next morning my cage was wrapped up while the children of the family stood around weeping. I was ready to weep myself, too, to tell you the truth. After I was all covered up the youngest one broke a hole in the top of my paper to say a last farewell to me. She dropped a couple of large tears on my head too. Then I felt myself being carried out into the yard.

" 'That's rather a joke,' chuckled the chaffinch"

"And so, after weeks and months of watching people arrive and depart from my inn, I, too, was to set forth by coach along the white road that led away to the horizon. Whither was I going? What adventures were in store for me? I fell to thinking of good old Jack. I wondered how his cheery face would look as he swung into the gate this evening to find my cage gone from the wall and no Pip to whistle 'Thank you' for his lump of sugar. Would he care very much, I asked myself. After all, to him I was only a canary—not even his canary at that. Oh, well, I thought, as the horses started forward with a jerk, it was no use being sentimental over it. I would face the future with a stout heart."

· The Third Chapter ·

AT THE MARQUIS'S CASTLE

I

T WAS a long journey. Sometimes I felt the coach going uphill, the horses panting, slowed to a walk. At other times we descended into valleys with the brakes creaking and groaning on the wheels. At last, after about seven hours of driving, we came to a halt and I heard the patter of hurrying feet. By the echoes, I gathered that we had passed into some kind of a courtyard or the stone portico to a big building. My cage was taken out and carried up a long, long winding flight of stairs.

"At length, on the wrapping paper being taken off, I found myself in a small, very beautifully furnished, round room. There were two people in it, the Marquis and a woman. The woman had a very nice face. She seemed sort of scared of the Marquis.

" 'Marjorie,' said he, 'I've brought you a present. This canary is a magnificent singer.'

" 'Thank you, Henry,' said she. 'It was very thoughtful of you.'

"And that was all. I could see there was something wrong. Marjorie was evidently the Marquis's wife. But after his being away from her for several days that was all she said: 'Thank you. It was very thoughtful of you.'

"After he had gone a cage was produced by the servants, the most elegant thing in cages you ever saw. It was made of solid silver. It had perches of carved ivory, food troughs of enameled gold, and a swing made of mother-of-pearl. As I was changed into it I wondered what other birds had lived in this gorgeous home and whether they had led happy lives.

"Well, after a few days at the castle I decided that I had not made such a bad move, after all. Fortune had again been kind. I was certainly treated royally. My cage was cleaned out scrupulously every day. A piece of apple was given me in the morning and a leaf of lettuce in the evening. The quality of the seed was the very best. I was given a silver pannikin of warm water to bathe in every other day. And altogether the care and service given me left nothing to be wished for.

"To all this, Marjorie, the Marquis's kind and gentle wife, herself attended—although she evidently had any number of servants to wait on her if she only rang the bell. I became very much attached to her. A thing that bothered me a good deal was that she did a lot of secret weeping. She was clearly very unhappy about something and I wondered what it was. You remember I had sworn I wouldn't sing a note if I was taken from the inn. And I didn't for over a week—much to the Marquis's disgust. He was all for sending me back to the inn when he found out that I hadn't sung since I had been in the castle. But his wife begged him to let her keep me, and he consented. That night, later, I saw her weeping again. And I felt so sorry for her that I suddenly started singing at the top of my voice to see if I could cheer her up. And sure enough, she raised her head and smiled and came and talked to me. After that I often sang to drive her tears away all the happy songs I knew, like 'Maids, Come Out; the Coach Is Here,' and the jingling harness currycomb song. But I wouldn't sing for the Marquis—not a note. And whenever he came into the room, if I was in the middle of a song, I'd stop at once.

"In that same small round room I lived all the time I was at the castle. It was apparently a special, letter-writing room, part of the private apartments of the Marquis's wife —or the Marchioness, as she was called. On warm days she would hang my cage on a nail outside the window, and from there I had a wonderfully fine view of the grounds and all the country for miles and miles around.

"One evening I got some idea of the thing—or one of the things—that was wrong between the Marquis and his wife. They had a long argument. It was all about the workmen in the mines and the mills. She wanted him to be kinder to them and to keep more of them working. But he said that with the new machinery he did not need even as many as he had. She told him that a lot of workmen's wives and children were starving. He said that wasn't his fault.

"Further, I gathered from this discussion that in one mine some distance away the workmen who had been dismissed had come back in a crowd and smashed the machines and wrecked the mine. Then soldiers had been called in, and many workers were shot and women left widows and children orphans. The Marchioness begged her husband on her knees to stop this kind of thing. He only laughed. The machines were bound to come, he said, to take men's places and do more work. In all the mills and mines throughout the country, machinery was being put in and idle men were opposing it. It was the march of time, he told her.

"After the Marquis had gone a letter came for the Marchioness. I could see her getting terribly agitated as she read it. She called in a trusted companion, a sort of secretary she had, and told her all about it. It was from a woman in one of the mill towns within the Marquis's lands. It told of the awful distress in the homes of idle workmen—starving children and whatnot. And that night the Marchioness dressed herself like a working woman and stole out of the castle grounds by the little orchard gate. I saw her from my window in the tower. With loaves of bread and foodstuffs in a basket, she went miles and miles on foot to find the woman who had written the letter. When she came back it was after two in the morning. And I, who had been left on my peg outside the window all that time, was nearly frozen in the chill morning air. She brought me in and wept over me when she discovered her forgetfulness. But I quite understood—and, anyway, it was the only time she had ever neglected me.

"Two days after that, news came in that another factory had had its machinery smashed. The Marquis was furious, though, as usual, he was very quiet and dignified and cold, even in his fury. He sent word for more soldiers to protect the mines and factories. And it seems that the same day that the soldiers arrived, one of the sergeants got into a quarrel with a workman. Before anybody knew what was happening a general battle had begun between the troops and the workers. When it was over it was found that one hundred and fifty workers had been killed.

"This caused a tremendous sensation and everybody was talking about it. I heard the servants who swept the room saying that this was war—that the Marquis had better look out. Powerful though he was, he couldn't shoot people down in crowds like dogs, they said. One maid there was who used to bring trays up from the kitchen to the Marchioness's little tower room. She had a brother among the workmen who had been killed. I remember her going off

"She brought me in and wept over me"

in tears to help her sister-in-law, who now had no husband. Many of the castle servants were for going with her, they were so indignant. They were talking angrily around the weeping maid on the front steps when suddenly the Marquis appeared from the garden. He asked them what was all the noise about. And so great was the respect and fear in which he was held that the group without a word melted away, leaving the maid all alone. The Marquis gave her several guineas and turned to go into the house. But the maid flung the money after him and screamed, 'I want my brother back, not your dirty money!'

"Then she fled, weeping, through the garden. It was the first time I had seen the Marquis openly defied.

"After that," Pippinella continued, "feeling began to run high. From all quarters came word that workmen were saying what they thought about the big fight—or slaughter, as they called it. Nearly all those who were employed to run machines went on strike out of sympathy for the relatives of those who had been killed. That, of course, made matters worse because even more wives and families went hungry than before.

"One morning I was sitting in my cage beside the tower window looking out at the peaceful woods down below, when I saw a man urging a panting horse up the hill toward the castle as fast as he could go. The Marchioness saw him also from the window and sent a maid down at once to find out what news the man brought. The maid returned in a few minutes in a great state of excitement and told her mistress that the whole countryside was up in arms. Thousands of workers, some from towns miles away, were marching toward the castle. The messenger had come to warn the Marquis that his life was in danger. Word had been sent to the soldiers, but no regiments were near enough to come to the rescue for some hours yet. The workers had been joined by many farmers on the Marquis's lands and now an army, thousands strong, was on its way here bent on mischief and destruction.

"Hearing this, the Marchioness ran downstairs at once to find her husband. When she was gone I heard a very peculiar noise from beyond the woods. It was a dull, low roar, coming nearer all the time, growing louder and louder. Presently I saw the Marquis and his wife in the garden at the foot of the tower. She was trying to persuade him to flee. At first he refused. But soon, as the howling army of workmen drew nearer, he consented and led the way toward the stables to get horses. The Marchioness had not gone many steps before she evidently remembered me. She stopped, pointed up at my cage, and said something to her husband. But he only took her by the wrist and dragged her on toward the stables. She looked back several times, but the Marquis wouldn't let her linger. Presently they disappeared from view around the hedge, and that was the last I ever saw of either of them.

"When finally the workmen came in sight they were certainly a strange army to behold. You never saw such a ragged, half-starved, wild-looking lot. At first they were afraid they might be fired on from the battlements and windows. And they approached cautiously, keeping within the cover of the woods.

"When the workmen saw there was no danger they gathered in hundreds and thousands in front of the castle, howling and swearing and singing songs, waving hammers and pitchforks. Some of the servants came out to join them. But the butler, an old, old man who had the keys, was determined to defend his master's property to the last. He locked the doors and barred the windows and would let no one in.

"But the leader of the workmen sent for a heavy beam. And with this as a battering ram they soon beat in the main door, drove the old butler out, and had the place to themselves.

"Then a crazy feast of destruction began. Bottles and barrels of wine were hauled up from the cellar, opened on the lawn, and drunk by the workmen. Costly silks, hangings, clocks, and furniture were thrown from the windows. Anything of value that wasn't smashed was stolen. They didn't come up the tower stairs as high as my room, but I could hear them in the rooms below me, laughing and roaring and breaking things with hammers.

"Looking downward into the castle forecourt again, I saw the leader calling to everyone to leave the building. I heard the men in the rooms below mine go clattering down the stairs. Soon I was the only one left in the castle. I wondered what this new move meant. When they were all gathered about him outside I saw the leader raise his hand for silence. He was going to tell them something. As the crazy mob grew quiet I strained my ears to catch his words. I heard them. And they almost made my heart stand still. For he was ordering them to bring straw from the stables and oil from the cellars. They were going to set the castle on fire!"

It was now quite late—long after midnight—and the sudden neighing of one of the horses from the nearby stables reminded the Doctor that the circus must open to the public at ten o'clock, as usual, tomorrow morning. So, in spite of the protests of Gub-Gub (who dearly loved any excuse for staying up late), the green canary was put in her cage and the Dolittle family circle was packed off to bed.

· The Fourth Chapter ·
THE RESCUE

THE following evening, after the crowds had left the circus inclosure and the sideshows had been closed up and everything put in shipshape for the night, Too-Too went over the accounts with the Doctor before supper, instead of after, so as to leave the evening free for the continuation of Pippinella's story. And as soon as Dab-Dab had cleared away the supper things the door of the little green canary's cage was opened, and she flew down onto the table and took her seat on the Doctor's tobacco box.

"All right," said John Dolittle, opening his notebook and taking a pencil from his pocket. "As soon as you are ready—"

"Just a minute," said Gub-Gub. "My chair's too low. I must get a cushion. I don't listen well when I'm not sitting high."

"Fusspot!" snorted Dab-Dab.

"Well," Pippinella began, "you can imagine how I felt— or rather you can't imagine it. No one could without being in my shoes. I really thought my last hour had come. I watched the crowd below in fascinated horror. I saw groups of men running between the front entrance of the

" 'I don't listen well when I'm not sitting high,' said Gub-Gub"

castle and the stable, bearing bales of straw. These they
piled against the great oak door, and some more inside the
main hall, all along the wooden paneling that ran around
the room. Then they brought up from the cellar jugs of oil,
cans of oil, barrels of oil. They soaked the straw with this
and threw more of it over the long curtains that were floating from the open windows in front of the castle.

"Then I saw the leader going around, getting all his men
out of the building before he set fire to it. He sent some

down into the woods—to be on the lookout for anyone's approach, I suppose. He was probably afraid of the soldiers' coming. For a moment there was a strange awed silence while the match was being put to the straw. It was clear that they all realized the seriousness of the crime they were committing. But as the bonfire flared up sudden and bright within the hall, a fiendish roar of delight broke from the ragged crew. And joining hands in a great ring, they danced a wild jig around the burning home of the man they hated.

"What horses were left in the stables had been taken out and tethered in safety among the trees some distance away. Even the Marquis's dogs, a Russian wolfhound and a King Charles spaniel, had been rescued and led out before the straw was lit. I alone had been overlooked. After the flame had taken well hold of the great oak doors and fire and smoke barred all admittance, some of the men at last caught sight of me, high up on the tower wall. For I saw several pointing up. But if they had wanted to save me then, it was too late. The paneling, the doors, the floors, the stairs—everything of wood in the lower part of the building was now a seething, roaring mass of flame.

"Waves of hot air, clouds of choking smoke, flurries of burning sparks swirled upward around my silver cage. The smoke was the worst. At first I thought I would surely be suffocated long before I was burned.

"But luckily, soon after the fire started a fitful breeze began. And every once in a while, when I thought I had reached my last gasp, the wind would sweep the rising smoke away to the side and give me a chance to breathe again.

"I pecked and tugged at the bars of my cage. Although I knew there wasn't the least possibility of my getting out, like a drowning man I still hoped that a lucky chance would show me something loose or weak enough to bend or break. But soon I saw I was merely wasting my strength in struggling. Then I started calling to whatever wild birds I saw flying in the neighborhood. But the swirling smoke terrified them so they were afraid to venture close. And even if they had, I doubt if there would have been anything they could have done to help me.

"From my position I could see inside the tower through the open window, as well as down onto the woods and all around outside. And presently, as I peered into the room, wondering if any help could come from that quarter, I saw a mouse run out into the middle of the floor in a great state of excitement.

" 'Where's the smoke coming from?' she cried. 'What's burning?'

" 'The castle's on fire,' I said. 'Come up here and see if you can gnaw a hole through this cage of mine. I'm going to be roasted if somebody doesn't let me out.'

" 'What do you think I am?' she said. 'A pair of pliers or a file? I can't eat through silver. Besides, I've got a family of five children down in my hole under the floor. I must look after them.'

"She ran to the door, muttering to herself, and disappeared down the winding stair. In a minute she was back again.

" 'I can't take them that way,' she said. 'Below the third landing the whole staircase is burning.'

"She sprang up onto the windowsill. It's funny how little details, in moments of great distress, stick in your mind. I remember exactly how she looked, not six inches from the wall of my cage, this tiny creature gazing over the lip of the stone windowsill, down from that tremendous height into the garden and the treetops far below. Her whiskers trembled and her nose twitched at the end. She wasn't concerned about me, shut up and powerless to escape—though goodness knows she had stolen my food often enough. All she was thinking of was those wretched little brats of hers in the nest beneath the floor.

" 'Bother it!' the mouse muttered. 'What a distance. Well, it's the only chance. I might as well begin.'

"And she turned around, sprang down into the room, shot across the floor, and disappeared into her hole. She wasn't gone more than a moment. When she showed up again she had a scrubby little pink baby in her mouth, without any fur on it yet and eyes still closed. It looked like a pig the size of a bean. She came to the edge of the sill and without the least hesitation started out on the face of the wall, scrambling her way along the mortar cracks between the stones. You'd think it would be impossible even for a mouse to make its way down the outside of a high tower like that. But the weather and rain had worn the joints deep in most places; and they have a wonderful way of clinging, have mice.

"I watched her get two-thirds of the way down, and then the heat and smoke of the fire below were too much for her. I saw her looking across at the tree, whose topmost boughs came close to the tower. She measured the distance with her eye. And still clutching her scrubby youngster in her teeth, she leapt. She just caught the endmost leaves with her claws. And the slender limb swayed gently downward with her weight. Then she scuttled along the bough, reached the trunk, dumped her child in some crack or crevice, and started back to fetch the rest.

"That mouse, to get each of her five children over that long trip, had a terrible lot of hard work ahead of her. As I watched her scrambling laboriously up the tower again,

"Still clutching her scrubby youngster in her teeth, she leapt"

disappearing in and out of the mortar cracks, an idea came to me.

"When she regained the windowsill I said to her, 'You've got four more to carry down. And the fire is creeping higher up the stairs every minute. If I were out of my cage I could fly down with them in a tenth of the time you'd take. Why don't you try to set me free?'

"I saw her glance up at me shrewdly with her little beady eyes.

" 'I don't trust canaries,' she said after a moment. 'And in any case there's no place in that cage that I could bite through.'

"And she ran off to her hole for another load.

"She was back even quicker than the first time.

" 'It's getting hot under the floor,' she said. 'And the smoke is already drifting through the joints. I think I'll bring all the children out onto the sill, so that they won't suffocate.'

"And she went and fetched the remainder of her precious family and laid them side by side on the stone beside my cage. Then, taking one at a time, she started off to carry them to safety. Four times I saw her descend that giddy zigzag trail of hers into the welter of smoke and sparks that seethed, denser and blacker every minute, about the base of the tower. And four more times she made that leap from the sheer face of the stonework, with a baby in her mouth, across the tips of the tree boughs. The leaves of these were now blackened and scorched with the high-reaching fire. On the third trip I saw that mouse actually jump through tongues of flames. But still she came back for the fourth. As she reached the sill for the last load she was staggering and weak, and I could see that her fur and whiskers had been singed.

"It was not many minutes after she had gone for good that I heard a tremendous crash inside the tower and a shower of sparks came up into the little round room. The long spiral staircase, or part of it, had fallen down. Its lower supports had been burnt away below. I sometimes think that that was the thing that saved me as much as anything else. Because it cut off my little room at the top from the burning woodwork lower down. If the fire had ever reached that room I would have been gone for sure. For although my cage was in the open air outside, it was much too close to the edge of the window to be safe. Below me I could now see flames pouring out of the windows, just as though they were furnace chimneys.

"I saw the leader of the workmen shout to his men to keep well back from the walls. They evidently expected the whole tower soon to crumble and fall down. That would mean the end for me, of course, because I would almost certainly fall right into the middle of the fire raging on the lower floors.

"In answer to their leader's orders the men were moving off among the trees, when I noticed that some new excitement had caught their attention. They began talking and calling to one another and pointing down the hill toward the foot of the woods. With the noise of the roaring fire I could hear neither what they said nor what it was they were so concerned about. Soon a sort of general panic broke out among them. For, gathering up what stolen goods they could carry, they scattered away from the castle, looking backward over their shoulders toward the woods as they ran. In two minutes there wasn't one of them left in sight. The mouse had gone. The men had gone. I was alone with the fire.

"And then suddenly, in a lull in the roaring of the flames, I heard a sound that brought hope back into my despairing heart. It was the rap-rap-rap, rap-a-tap, tap, tap of a drum.

"I sprang to my perch and craned my neck to look out over the woods. And there, winding toward me, up the road, far, far off, like a thin red ribbon, were soldiers marching in fours!

"By the time the soldiers reached the castle the smoke coming up from below was so bad that I could see only occasionally with any clearness at all. I was now gasping and choking for breath and felt very dizzy in the head. I managed to make out, however, that the officer in charge was dividing his men into two parties. One, which he took command of himself, went off in pursuit of the workmen. The other was left behind to put out the fire. But the castle, of course, was entirely ruined. Shortly after they arrived one of the side walls of the main hall fell in with a crash, and a large part of the roof came down with it. Yet my tower still stood.

"There was a large fish pond not far from the front door. And the soldiers got a lot of buckets from the stables and formed a chain, handing the water up to some of their companions, who threw it on the fire.

"Almost immediately the heat and smoke rising around my cage began to lessen. But, of course, it took hours of this bucket work to get the fire really under control.

"The officer with the other party returned. He had caught no one. Some of his men held the horses, which they had found tied among the trees. These and some provisions in the cellars and a few small outhouses were all of that magnificent property to be saved. And it had been one of the finest castles in the country, famous for its beauty the world over.

"The officer, seeing there was nothing more he could do, now left a sergeant in charge and, taking one of the soldiers with him, went back down the road leading through the woods. The rest continued with the work of fighting the fire and making sure that it did not break out again.

"As soon as my ears had caught the cheerful beating of that drum I had started singing. But on account of the smoke my song had been little more than coughs and splutters. Now, however, with the air cleared, I opened my throat and let go for all I was worth, 'Maids, Come Out, the Coach Is Here.' And the old sergeant, who was superintending the soldiers' work, lifted his head and listened. He couldn't make out where the sound was coming from. But presently he caught sight of my cage, way, way up at the top of the blackened tower.

" 'By Jove, boys!' I heard him cry. 'A canary! The sole survivor of the garrison. Let's get him for good luck.'

"But getting me was no easy matter. Piles of fallen stonework now covered every entrance. Then they searched the stables for a ladder. They found one long enough to reach the lowest of the tower windows. But the soldier who scaled up it called down to his companions that the staircase inside was gone, and he could get no higher. Nevertheless, the old sergeant was determined to get me.

"The sergeant was convinced that I, who had come through such a fire and could still sing songs, would bring luck to any regiment. And he swore a tremendous oath that he would get me down or break his neck. Then he went back to the stable and got some ropes and himself ascended the ladder to the bottom window of the tower. By throwing the rope over broken beams and other bits of ruined woodwork that still remained within, he hauled himself upward little by little. And finally I saw his funny face appear through the hole in the floor of my room where the staircase had been. He had a terrible scar across his cheek, from an old wound, I suppose. But it was a nice face, for all that.

" 'Hulloa, my lad!' said he, hoisting himself into the room and coming to the window. 'So you're the only one who stood by the castle, eh? By the hinges of hell, you're a real soldier, you are! You come and join the Fusiliers, Dick. And we'll make you the mascot of the regiment.'

"As my rescuer stuck his head out of the window to lift my cage off its nail, his companions down below sent up a cheer. He fastened his rope to the silver ring of the cage and started to lower me down the outside of the tower. I descended slowly, swinging like the pendulum of some great clock from that enormous height. And finally I landed safe on solid earth in the midst of a crowd of cheering soldiers.

"And that is how another chapter in my life ended—and still another began."

· The Fifth Chapter ·
THE MIDGET MASCOT

AND THUS I became a soldier—the mascot of the Fusiliers. There are not many canaries who can boast of that—that they have traveled with the troops, taken part in battles and skirmishes, and led a regular military life."

"Well, I've led a sailor's life," said Gub-Gub, "—sailed all around the world, and without getting seasick, too."

"Never mind that, now," said the Doctor. "Let Pippinella get on with her story."

"Those soldiers," the canary continued, "had no love for the Marquis. They had been ordered to come to the rescue of his home, and they had obeyed. But their hearts were more with the workers in this struggle. And I think they must have known that he was already dead when they arrived at the castle, or they would never have dared to take me just the way they did. As a matter of fact, he had been killed outside the next town. The Marchioness, who had always been so kind to the poor, of course was not molested. But the whole thing saddened her dreadfully, and she went abroad right away and remained there the rest of her days.

"My beautiful silver cage was sold by one of the soldiers

(they were afraid to keep it, of course, lest it be recognized as the Marquis's property) and I was changed into a plain one of wood. That old sergeant with the funny scarred face took me under his own particular care and protection. He had my new wooden cage enameled red, white, and blue. The crest of the regiment was painted on the side, and ribbons were hung on the corners to make it even still gayer.

"Well—it's funny—those men were convinced that I bore a charmed life. The story of how they found me singing in the burning castle was told over and over and over again. And each time it was retold an extra bit was added on to it to make it just a little more wonderful. I came to be regarded with an almost sacred importance. It was believed that nothing could kill me, and that so long as I was with the Fusiliers the regiment must have good luck. I remember once, when I was ill—just an ordinary case of colic, you know, nothing serious—those soldiers stood around my cage in droves for hours on end, with the most woebegone expression on their faces you ever saw. They were terrified, just terrified, that I was going to die. And when I finally got well and started to sing again, they cheered and bellowed songs the whole night through to celebrate my recovery.

"Once in a skirmish two bullets went right through my cage, one smashing my water pot, the other carrying away the very perch I was standing on. When the fight was over and this was discovered, my cage was handed right around the whole regiment, to show everybody the proof (as they thought it) that I did indeed have a charmed life and could not be killed. Those funny, funny men spoke in whispers, almost as though they were in church, as they took my cage in their horny hands and gazed with reverent wonder at the smashed perch, the broken water pot, and me hopping around unharmed.

"That night they went through the ceremony of giving me a medal for distinguished conduct under fire. A whole platoon of them lined up and presented arms while my old sergeant hung the decoration on the corner of my cage. The next day the commanding officer got to hear of it and I was sent for and carried to the officers' mess, where everything was very grand and elegant. The colonel and the major and the adjutant listened while the old sergeant recited the record of my military career. But when they asked him where he had got me from, he suddenly blushed and became all embarrassed. Finally he blurted out the truth and told them of my rescue from the fire. The colonel frowned and said something about looting. But finally he agreed to let the man keep me till he had written to the Marchioness and got her consent—which later she willingly gave. Then the adjutant pointed to the medal hanging on my cage and they all laughed. The major said that even if I'd begun by being stolen, I was surely the only canary who ever had been decorated for distinguished conduct under fire and that any regiment ought to be proud to claim me as a mascot.

"Well, it was a funny life, the army. I had always thought that if you were a soldier of course you spent most of your time fighting. I was astonished to find that you don't. You spend the greater part of it polishing buttons. Polishing with the military is a perfect passion. If it isn't buttons, it's belt buckles or bayonets or gun barrels or shoes. Even on my cage they found something to polish. A small drummer boy was given the job of shining up the little brass feet on the bottom of it every morning—and a great nuisance he was, shaking and joggling me all over the place when I wanted to get my breakfast in peace.

"My old sergeant hung the decoration on the corner of my cage"

"I used to love the marching and I always had a real thrill when I heard the bugler blowing the fall-in, for it often meant that we were moving off to new scenes and new adventures. I used to travel with the little baggage cart that carried the cooking implements and other paraphernalia in the rear. And as they always put my cage on the top of everything I was quite high up and in a splendid position to see all there was to be seen. The men used to sing songs to cheer themselves upon long, tiresome marches. And I, too, made up a marching song of my own and sang it always when I saw them getting tired and hot and weary:

> Oh, I'm the midget mascot,
> I'm a feathered Fusilier,

it began. And then I put a lot of twiddly bits, trills, cadenzas, and runs to imitate the piping of the drum-and-fife band. It was one of the best musical compositions I ever did. There was a real military swing to it and it had four hundred and twenty-five verses, so as to last through a good, long march. The men just loved it. And as I watched them trudging down the road ahead of me I again felt that I was taking an active part, even though a small one, in the lives of men.

"Shortly after I joined the Fusiliers our regiment was ordered to proceed at once to an outbreak in a region to the north, and we started off. At inns and villages along the road we were told that one of the factory towns at which we would shortly arrive was entirely in the hands of the rioting workers. They had heard of our coming and were preparing to give us a hot reception. But our soldiers slipped in among the houses and in less than an hour after the fight began, more than half of the workers' guns had been captured. The crews of these captured guns usually escaped. For the soldiers, who were doing their work with as little slaughter as possible, let them go without firing at them whenever they did not actually stand and fight.

"When the battle was over it was discovered that nearly all the fighting workmen had retired to a big mine in the western half of the town. In the buildings of this and in a large factory alongside it they were going to make a last stand against the soldiers and die rather than be captured.

But it didn't work out that way. When my Fusiliers were ordered to fire on the buildings they deliberately aimed the guns so that the cannonballs whistled harmlessly over the roofs. Again and again this was repeated until the general was livid with rage.

"By this time the workers inside the buildings, watching through loopholes, had realized that the soldiers were inclined to side with them. And while the general broke out into another tirade and confusion reigned, they suddenly opened the doors of the buildings and rushed forward toward the square at top speed.

"Well, in the end, my gallant Fusiliers were defeated by a crowd of ragged workmen, half of them without arms of any kind. But of course they wanted to be defeated. Rather than be compelled to fire cannons on unfortified buildings full of their fellow countrymen they were quite willing, for once in their lives, to be taken prisoners. I heard afterward that they were sent abroad to more regular warlike fighting, where there would be no danger of their sympathizing with the enemy.

"In the meantime the baggage wagon on which my cage was tied was treated as the booty of war. And I suddenly found myself taken over by a couple of very dirty men and trundled out of the square, down some winding streets that seemed to be leading into the workmen's quarters of the town.

"My short but brilliant military career was over."

As Pippinella came to the end of this part of her story Dab-Dab began to bustle around busily making preparations for bed. Although she enjoyed every word of the canary's account of her life, Dab-Dab was the practical one. She had to keep an eye on the Doctor and his family else they would sit up the whole night.

"Time for bed!" she said firmly. "Tomorrow's another day—and a busy one."

Then the Doctor and his family began tucking themselves away for the night. Too-Too perched high on a shelf in a dark corner of the caravan, Whitey curled up in the pocket of an old jacket that belonged to the Doctor, and Jip lay on a mat folded under the Doctor's bed.

Pippinella, of course, returned to her cage, which hung on a hook near the window of the wagon; and Dab-Dab, after seeing that everyone was comfortable and that the lights were out, waddled off to a small nestlike bed the Doctor had fixed out of an empty wooden crate.

"I'm hungry!" wailed Gub-Gub from his place beside the vegetable bin. "These turnips smell so good it keeps me awake."

"Sh-sh-sh!" whispered Dab-Dab. "There'll be no eating around here until morning!"

· The Sixth Chapter ·
THE FORTUNES OF WAR

MY CAPTORS were evidently in a hurry," began Pippinella the next evening when the Doctor and his animals had settled themselves to hear the continuation of her story. "It was growing dark and the baggage wagon was pushed over the jolting, cobbly streets on the run.

"I think that these men who ran off with the regimental cart must have thought that it contained food. Because when they came to a quiet corner of the street they stopped and felt through the inside of it. I heard them cursing in the dark when their groping hands touched nothing but pots and pans and spare harness. And after they had put me back and hurried on I saw their faces in the glimmer of a streetlamp, and the poor fellows looked dreadfully pinched and thin.

"I then supposed that their intention was to sell me and the wagon to get money to buy food with. And I was right. After they had gone a little farther we turned into a narrow alley, passed under an archway, and came into a big, big hall. It seemed to be some kind of factory workshop, and the place was jammed with workers. It was dimly lighted with only a few candles and sputtering torches. The men

"The baggage wagon was pushed over the jolting,
cobbly streets on the run"

were gathered in groups, talking in low voices, with their
heads together. When my fellows pushed open the doors
and entered, all the whispering ceased. The crowd turned
and glared at us.

"As soon as we were admitted the door was carefully
locked and barred. And then I noticed that all the windows
were covered with wooden shutters, so that the lights
could not be seen from outside. And all of a sudden it

dawned on me that I had been brought to the mine, or the big factory alongside of it, and that this was one of the buildings that the general had commanded the Fusiliers to bombard. I began to wonder how long it would be before he would have other troops brought to the town who would not hesitate to fire cannonballs into crowded factories.

"As soon as the barring of the door had been attended to, the men thronged around my little cart and started to claw through it to see what it contained. Suddenly a big man, who seemed to be a leader, ordered them in a rough voice to leave it alone. They fell back, evidently much afraid of him. Something in the man's face struck me as familiar and I began to cudgel my brain to think where I had seen him before. And then in a flash I remembered: It was the same man who had led the workers in their attack on the Marquis's castle.

"He went through the cart himself and told the disappointed crowd that it contained no food.

" 'Then let's sell it and buy some,' cried the men.

"But as it clearly would not bring enough to buy food for all of them, it was finally agreed that lots should be drawn and that the winner should get the cart.

" 'And what about the canary?' called one. 'Likely a man could get as much for him as for the old truck and all the pans put together.'

" 'All right,' said the leader. 'Then draw lots for the bird separate. We'll put two marked papers in the hat—one for the cart and one for the canary. The first winner gets his choice; the second gets what's left; and the rest get nothing.'

" 'Aye, aye!' called the crowd. 'That's fair enough.'

" 'Sh!' hissed the leader. 'Not so loud! How do we know who's sneaking around outside? I don't trust them bloomin' Fusiliers—even though they did give in so easy. Talk low, talk low!'

"So my next experience was to have a lot of ragged workers draw lots for me. As I saw them crowding around the hat that contained bits of paper, I wondered which of them I would fall to. Some of them looked hungry and wild enough to cook me and eat me. The prospects for the future were not pleasing.

"One by one they began picking out their bits of paper. Five, ten, fifteen opened them—and with a grunt of disgust threw them on the floor. It seemed to be taking hours of time, but of course it was really only minutes.

"At length a cry announced that a lucky ticket had been drawn. The owner brought it, smiling, to the leader and showed a rough cross in pencil on it.

" 'Well, that gives you the first choice,' said the big man. 'Which are you going to take, the cart or the canary?'

"The other, a thin fellow with a limp, looked from the wagon to me and back to the wagon again. I didn't like his face.

" 'The cart,' he said at last, to my great delight.

"Another cry. A second lucky ticket had been drawn. I craned my neck to peer over the crowd and get a glimpse of the man's face. I finally saw him and my heart lifted. Although his cheeks were lined and gaunt with hunger, it was a kind face.

" 'The canary's yours,' said the big man, handing him my cage. 'And that's the end of the show.'

"The winner took my cage in his hands and left the building. The question of food interested us both at this point more than anything else. Heaven only knows how long he had been going on half rations or less, and I had had no seed or water all day. As we went along I saw lots of autumn seed on weeds and wild flowers that would have made good eating for me—if only I could get at it. He, of course, not knowing what wild seeds are edible for canaries, couldn't help me. He did, however, stop by a stream and fill my water bowl for me, which I was mighty glad of. And later he found some groundsel growing among the standing corn, and that, too, he gave me. I still felt pretty hungry, but far less so than I had been.

"After he had come near to a farmhouse he hid my cage under a hedge and went forward to the door to ask for food for himself. The farmer's wife took pity on his haggard and hungry looks, and she gave him a good square meal of bread and cold meat. He brought back a small crust when he came to fetch me and stuck it between the bars of my cage. It was a good homemade bread, and I could have eaten two more of the same size.

"So, both of us fortified with food, we set out to do the ten miles that lay between us and the mining town that he was making for. It was a pleasant, sunny morning. And something of the sadness with which the grim night had weighed me down left my spirits as the man strode forward in the fresh early air, with my cage beneath his arm. He, too, seemed in cheerier mood. We were now upon a main highway running north and south. Wagons and carriages passed us occasionally, going either way. I hoped that one of these would offer us a ride, because traveling in a cage under a man's arm is not the most comfortable kind of journeying by a great deal. And, sure enough, after we had tramped along for about half an hour, the driver of a covered cart—a sort of general grocer's wagon—stopped and asked if we would like a lift. He was going to the town we were bound for, and I was delighted when my man put me in the back among the groceries and got up himself beside the driver.

"As it happened, my cage had been placed right next to a

"It didn't take more than a moment for me to peck a hole
through the covering"

packet of oatmeal. I smelled it through the paper bag. And
of course it didn't take more than a moment for me to peck
a hole through the covering, and I helped myself to a thim-
bleful of the grocer's wares. I felt sort of mean doing it to
the man who was giving us a free ride. But it was only a
very tiny quantity I took—not enough for anyone to miss
—and I hadn't tasted grain of any kind in over twenty-four
hours.

"My man chatted with the grocer as we drove. And I gathered from the conversation that he had a brother, who was also a miner at this town we were coming to. Apparently it was his intention to stay at his house, if there was room, till he got a job in the mines.

"If I had known," Pippinella continued in rather a sadly reminiscent voice, "what sort of life I was coming to, I wouldn't have been half as cheerful over that journey, in spite of the nice, fresh morning. I had for some time now been among miners. But I didn't yet know anything whatever of their homes, their lives, or their work."

· The Seventh Chapter ·
THE COAL MINE

THE FIRST impression that I got of the town as we approached it was anything but encouraging. There had been no rioting here and work was proceeding as usual. For more than a mile outside all the grass and trees seemed sort of sick and dirty. The sky over the town was murky with smoke from the tall chimneys and foundries and factories. On every spare piece of ground, instead of a statue or a fountain or a garden, there was a messy pile of cinders, scrap iron, junk, or furnace slag. I wondered why men did this; it did not seem to me that all the coal and all the steel in the world was worth it—ruining the landscape in this way.

"And they didn't seem any happier for it. I looked at their faces as we passed them, trudging down the streets to work in the early morning. Their clothes were all black and sooty, their faces pale and cheerless. They carried little tin boxes in their hands, which contained their lunches, to be eaten in the mines or at the factory benches.

"In the middle of the town my man got down from the cart, took me out, and thanked the driver for his ride. Then he went off through some narrow streets, where all the houses seemed alike—plain, ugly red brick—and finally knocked on a door.

"A pale-faced untidy woman answered it, with three dirty children clinging to her skirts. She greeted him and invited him to come in. We passed to the back of the house into a small kitchen. The whole place smelled terribly of bad cooking. The woman went on with washing some clothes, at which she had evidently been interrupted, and the man sat down and talked with her. In the meantime the children poked their jammy fingers through the bars of my cage, which had been placed upon the table among a lot of dirty dishes. I was afraid they were going to upset it while the man was busy talking, so I pecked one on the hand, just slightly, to warn him to be careful. He immediately burst into howls. Then my cage was taken and hung up in the window, where I got an elegant view of two ash barrels and a brick wall.

" 'Good Lord,' I thought to myself, 'is this what I've come to? Such a home! What a life!'

"In the evening the brother returned from work, covered with coal grit, tired, and weary. He washed his face in the kitchen sink while the newcomer told him how he had left his own town and journeyed hither, seeking work. The brother said he would speak to the foreman and try to get him a job in the same mine he worked in.

"Then they had supper. Ordinarily the cheerful noise of knives and forks and dishes would have made me sing. It always did in the castle when the Marchioness took her meals with me in the little tower room. And so it did with the soldiers when they all sat around my baggage cart and rattled their little tin dishes and drank soup with a hissing noise like horses. But somehow here in this squalid, smelly room among these tired, dirty people, I just couldn't sing. I almost felt as though I'd never be able to sing again.

"She greeted him and invited him to come in"

"And after the woman had put some broken rice and bread crumbs into my seed trough I ate a little, put my head under my wing to shut out the picture of that wretched room, and miserably went to sleep.

"Well, my man got his job. And two days later he started out with his brother to go to work in the morning; and he returned with him in the evening. And, supposing that I was going to be here for some time, I tried to settle down and take an interest in the household and in the family.

But I found it very hard work. Their conversation was so dull, what there was of it. In the morning the men got up, leaving only time enough to gobble their breakfast and rush off to work. In the evening the poor fellows were so tired that they went to bed almost immediately after supper. And in between all I had to listen to was the children bawling and the woman scolding them.

"Many a time I'd say to myself: Look here, my girl, this won't do. You must cheer up. Laugh at your troubles and sing a song.

"And then I'd throw my head back and try to fool myself that I was out in the green woods, all merry and bright. But before I'd sing more than two notes one of the brats would start crying, or the harassed mother would interrupt with some complaint. It was no use. I just couldn't sing in that house.

"After I'd been there a week I gathered from the conversation of the men one evening that I was going to be taken somewhere the following day. I was delighted. For I thought to myself that, no matter where it was, the change couldn't be for the worse.

"But I was wrong. Where do you suppose I was taken? You could never guess. I was taken down into the coal mine. I didn't know at the time that it was customary to keep canaries in coal mines. It seems that there is a very dangerous kind of gas, called coal damp, that sometimes comes out underground and kills the men working there if they are not warned in time to escape. The idea of having canaries down there is, apparently, that the birds being higher up than the men—hung on the walls of the passages —will get the gas first. Then if the birds start to suffocate the men are warned that it is time to get out of the mine. While the canaries are lively and hopping about they know it's all right.

"Well, I had never seen the inside of a coal mine before. And I hope I never will again. Of all the dreadful places to work and live, I think that must be the worst. My cage was taken by my owner and his brother the next morning, and we walked a good mile before we came to the mouth of the pit. Then we got into a sort of a big box with a rope to it. And wheels began to turn and we went down and down and down and down. The sun could not be seen. For light the men had little lamps fastened to their hats. The box stopped and we got out and went along a long, narrow passage that had little rails with wagons on them, running the length of it. Into these little wagons the coal was put, way back in the inside of the mine. Then it was trundled along till it came to the big shaft, where the sliding box, or lift, took it up to the top.

"After we had gone a good distance underground the men stopped, and my owner hung my cage on a nail high up on a wall of the passage. There they left me and went to their work. And all day long men passed and repassed with little wagons of coal, while others picked with pick axes and loaded the trucks with shovels. Again I was taking an active part in the lives of men. Such lives, poor wretches! My job was to wait for gas—to give warning, by coughing or choking or dying, that the deadly coal damp was stealing down the corridors to poison them.

"At first I feared I was going to be left there all night after the men went home. But I wasn't. When a whistle blew at the end of the day I was taken down from the wall, back to the sliding box, and up into the open air—and so home to the kitchen and the squalling children. It was now late in the fall and the daylight was short. It was barely dawn when we went to work in the morning and dark again before we came up at night. The only sunlight we saw was on Saturday afternoon and Sunday. I had been a hotel coach announcer; I had been a Marchioness's pet in a silver cage; I had been a crack regiment's mascot. Now I was a miner, working nine hours a day—sniffing for gas! It's a funny world.

"This was, I think, the unhappiest part of my life. Whatever change fate brought along, it was bound to be an improvement."

"But in the mine," Dab-Dab put in, "weren't you always in continued dread of this horrible gas poisoning you?"

"At the beginning, yes, I was," said Pippinella. "But after I had my first experience of it I was not so scared. I had supposed that if the gas ever did come while I was there that, of course, would be the end of me. But I was wrong. We had several goes of it in my mine, but no fatal accidents. I remember the first one especially. It was a little after noon, and the men had only been working about half an hour since lunch. I noticed a peculiar odor. Not knowing what gas smelled like, I didn't at first suspect what it was. It got stronger and stronger. Then suddenly my head began to swim and I thought, Gosh! this is it, sure enough! And I started to squawk and flutter about the cage and carry on like crazy. There were men working not more than seven or eight feet from my cage. But with the noise of their own shovels and picks they did not hear me. And their heads, of course, being lower than mine, they had not yet smelled the gas, which always floats to the top of a room first.

"After a couple of minutes had gone by and still they hadn't taken any notice of me, things began to look pretty bad. The beastly stuff was all in my nose and throat now, choking me, so I could hardly squeak at all. But still I kept on fluttering madly about the cage, even though I couldn't see where I was going. And just at the last minute, when everything was getting sort of dreamy in my head, the men put down their shovels and picks to take a rest. And in a voice that sounded all sort of funny and far away I heard one of them cry, 'Bill—Look at the bird! Gas!'

"Then that single word *Gas!* was shouted up and down the passages of the whole mine. Tools were dropped with a clatter on the ground; and the men, bending down to keep their heads low, started running for the hoist shaft. My man Bill leapt up and snatched my cage from the wall and fled after them.

"At the shaft we found hundreds of workers gathered, waiting their turn to go up in the sliding box. The whistle up at the top was blowing away like mad to warn any stray men who might still be lingering in the passages.

"When everyone had reached the open air, big suction fans were set to work to draw the gas out of the mine before the men would go to work again. It took hours to get all the passages cleared and safe. And we did not go down again that day.

"And then I realized that these men were taking the same risk as I was. After that first time, when we nearly got caught and suffocated, they were more careful. And at least one of the workers always kept an eye on my cage. If I showed the least sign of choking or feeling queer, they would give the alarm and clear out of the mine.

"The winter wore on. Sadly I often wondered how long I was to be a miner. For the first time since I had been a fledgling in the nest I fell to envying the wild birds again. What did it matter how many enemies you had, hawks, shrikes, cats, and whatnot, so long as you had liberty? The wild birds were free to sweep the skies: I lived under the ground—in a cage. I often thought of what my mother had told me of foreign birds—birds of paradise and gay-plumed macaws that flitted through jungles hung with orchids, in far-off tropical lands. Then I'd look around at the black coal walls of this underground burrow, at the lights on the men's caps glimmering in the gloom; and it seemed to me that one day of freedom in India, Africa, or Venezuela would be a good exchange for a whole life such as mine. Was I here for the rest of my days? Nine hours of work; home; to bed; and back to work again. Would the end never come?

"And at last it did. You know a canary is a somewhat smaller creature than a human being, but his life and what happens in it are just as important for him. Only, that of the two, the canary is the better philosopher. I've often thought that if a man or a woman had had my job in that mine, he or she would probably have pined away and died from sheer boredom and misery. The way I endured it was by just refusing to think too much. I kept saying to myself, Something must happen some day. And whatever it is, it'll be something new.

"One morning at eleven o'clock a party of visitors came to look over the mine. You wouldn't think, if you had ever worked in a coal mine, that anybody would want to go and look at one. But folks will do all sorts of things out of curiosity. And these people came to inspect us and our mine in rather the way they'd go to a zoo.

"The manager himself came down first to announce their coming. He asked the foreman of the gang in which my owner worked to see that the visitors were shown everything and were treated politely. And a little later the party itself arrived. There were about six of them altogether, ladies and gentlemen. They all wore long coats, which the manager had lent them, to protect their fine clothes from the coal dust and dirt. They were greatly impressed by things that to us miners were ordinary,

"She was the first in the party to notice me"

everyday matters. And many were the sarcastic remarks the workers made beneath their breath as these fastidious folks poked around and asked stupid questions.

"Among them was an old lady, a funny, fussy old thing, with a plain but very kind face. She was the first in the party to notice me.

" 'Good gracious!' she cried. 'A canary! What's he doing here?'

" 'He's for the gas, ma'am,' said the foreman.

"And then, of course, she wanted to know what that meant and the foreman told her all about it.

" 'Good gracious!' she kept saying. 'I had no idea they had canaries in coal mines. How very interesting! But how dreadful for the poor birds! Can I buy this one? I'd love to have a canary who had lived in a coal mine.'

"My heart jumped. The chance had come at last, a chance to get back into the open air—to a decent life!

"A long talk began between the old lady and the foreman and my owner. My owner said I was an especially good bird for gas, very sensitive and gave warning at the first traces. But the old lady seemed very determined. She really wanted to help me, I think, to give me a better kind of life. But she was also greatly attracted by the idea of having a bird who had lived in a real coal mine—as a sort of souvenir, perhaps. Also she seemed to have a good deal of money. Because every time my owner shook his head she would offer him a higher price. Till finally she got to ten guineas. Still he refused, and still the old lady went on higher. The workmen stood around listening, gaping with interest. But they weren't half so interested as I was. For on the result of this bargaining, my life, or at least my happiness, depended.

"At last, when the bidding had gone to twelve guineas, my owner gave in. I suppose I ought to have felt very proud, for it was a tremendous sum for a canary to cost. But I was much too busy feeling glad to have time for any other kind of sentiment.

"My cage was taken down from the wall and handed to the old lady. She gave the man her address—where he was to come the following day to get his money.

" 'Is it a cock? Does it sing?' she asked.

" 'I don't know, ma'am,' said the man. 'I understood it is

a cock. But he hasn't sung a single note since he's been with me.'

" 'I'd like to know who would—here,' growled one of the miners.

" 'Well, I'll take him anyway,' said the woman. 'I daresay he'll sing when he gets into the air and sunlight.'

"And so ended another chapter in the story of my adventures. For when the old lady, with the rest of the party, took me up in the sliding box I left the life of a miner behind me for good. I often thought afterward of those poor wretches toiling away underground and wondered how the other canary got along who took my place. But, oh my, I was glad that for me it was all over, and some new kind of a life was in sight!"

"I should think so!" declared the Doctor. "I've always felt terribly sorry for canaries who were forced to do such disagreeable work."

"Why must they use birds?" asked Whitey. "Wouldn't cats do just as well? I'm sure it would be a great relief to know that some of them were shut up in the mines."

The Doctor laughed at the mouse's remark.

"Yes, Whitey," he said. "For a mouse or a bird that *would* be a comfort. But, you see, birds—especially canaries—have a very sensitive respiratory system. They can detect the faintest odor of gas while any other animal would be unconscious of its presence."

Then the Doctor closed his notebook for the night.

"Dab-Dab," he said. "Could we have some cocoa and toast before we go to bed? I feel a bit hungry. How about the rest of you?"

"Hurray!" cried Gub-Gub. "There's nothing I like better than cocoa and toast—unless it's cauliflower."

"Cauliflower!" howled Jip. "That horrible stuff! I'd rather eat horseradish root!"

"That's good, too!" said Gub-Gub, smacking his lips.

"Well, there's not going to be any cauliflower—or horse-radish root," snapped Dab-Dab. "It will be cocoa and toast —as the Doctor ordered—*or nothing!*"

So they all sat down to steaming cups of cocoa and heaps of hot buttered toast, which they finished to the last drop and crumb. Pippinella, remembering the happy days that followed her miserable sojourn in the mines, sang them a tender lullaby which she had composed while living at Aunt Rosie's house.

· The Eighth Chapter ·
AUNT ROSIE'S HOUSE

AT THE MOUTH of the pit," Pippinella began the next evening, "there was a sort of cab or hired coach waiting for the old lady. And into this she put me and got in herself. And then we drove a long, long way through the country. I saw at once that she was a kind person but dreadfully fussy and particular. She kept moving my cage from one part of the cab to another.

" 'Little birdie musn't be in a draft,' she would say. And she'd take me off the seat and put me on the floor. But two minutes later she'd lift me up onto her lap.

" 'Little birdie getting enough air down there?' she'd ask. 'Tweet-tweet! Like to sit on Aunt Rosie's lap and look out of the window? See the corn sprouting in the pretty fields? Doesn't that look nice after living in a coal mine, little birdie?'

"And it did look nice, even though Aunt Rosie's chatter was tiresome and sort of silly. She meant well. And nothing could have spoiled the beauty of the country for me that morning. Spring was in the air. I had lived through the winter underground, and now when my release had come the hedges were budding and the crops showing

"She'd lift me onto her lap"

green in the plowed furrows. Out of the carriage window I saw birds hurrying here and there, in pairs, looking for places to build their nests. I hadn't talked to another bird in months and months. Somehow, for almost the first time since I had left my parents, I felt lonely for company of my own kind. I started to figure out exactly how long it was since I had spoken to another bird. But I was interrupted by Aunt Rosie speaking again.

" 'Little birdie sing a song? Tweet-tweet!'

"And then it flashed upon me that I had been practically dumb ever since I left the Fusiliers. I had sung them my marching song as they tramped to the town where all the fighting had been. I wondered if without practice in so long my voice was still any good at all.

" 'Little birdie sing a song?' Aunt Rosie repeated.

"With a flourish of wings I sprang to the top perch and threw back my head to begin 'The Midget Mascot,' but just at that moment two more birds, a thrush and his wife, sped by the carriage window with bits of dried grass hanging from their mouths.

"I've never built a nest, I thought to myself. It's spring, and I'm tired of being alone. It must be lots of fun to have a whole family of youngsters to bring up. Aunt Rosie doesn't know whether I'm a cock or a hen. If I sing then I'm a cock, so far as she's concerned. But if I don't maybe she'll decide I'm a hen and get me a mate. Then I'll build me a nest the way mother and father used to do. It's worth trying anyway. All right, I'll stay dumb for a while longer.

"The town to which the old lady brought me in her cab was very different from the one we had left. In this town all was peace and leisured, comfortable life. The old, old cathedral rose in the center of it, gray against the sky, and choughs and crows circled round it and built their nests in the belfry tower. There were lots of nice gardens and old houses, substantial and well built—and all different styles.

"Aunt Rosie's house had a fine garden at the back. When my cage was first hung in the window I noticed two peculiar things. One was that the other window in the room had a small mirror fixed outside of it on a little bracket. I wondered what this was for at first. But later on, when the old lady sat in her armchair and did her knitting, I saw that it was for watching the neighbors in. From where she sat she could see in the mirror who was coming down the

"My cage was hung in the window"

street. Several houses across the way had similar arrangements fixed outside the windows. Apparently watching the neighbors pass while you did your needlework was a favorite occupation in this town. It was the kind of town where folks had time to sit at their windows.

"The other thing that I observed was a streetlamp outside, close to the wall of Aunt Rosie's house. It was not more than a few feet from the bottom of my cage. And every evening an old lamplighter would hobble around with a ladder and climb up and light this lamp, and in the very early morning he'd come and put it out. The light used to shine right into the room—even through the blind. It kept me awake the first few nights—until the old lady noticed that it disturbed me. Then she always put the cover over my cage as soon as the streetlamp was lit. She embroidered a special one herself, made of heavy dark stuff, so that the light wouldn't shine through.

"I made a number of quite interesting friends while I stayed at Aunt Rosie's house. And the hobbling lamplighter was one of them. I never talked to him. But his arrival every night and morning was a regular and pleasant thing to make a note of. Life generally here moved along regular and pleasant lines.

"The old lady had lots of friends, all women. Several times a week they would come in to take tea with her, and they always brought their sewing with them. And to every new lot that came Aunt Rosie told the story over again of how she had bought me out of a coal mine, way down under the earth. Then they'd gather round my cage and gaze at me, openmouthed with awe.

"All through this I still kept mum and never a note did I sing, though often enough I felt like it, with the shade trees growing greener every day on the street outside and spring coming on in leaps and bounds. It was a nice place I had come to. But I wanted company of my own kind. And I was determined I wouldn't sing till the old lady got me a mate.

"It was on one of these sewing-circle occasions that a very peculiar incident occurred. Aunt Rosie was telling my story to a new group of women friends when one of them stepped forward and peered closely at me through the bars of my cage. Although her face seemed familiar I couldn't, at first, remember where I'd seen her before. But suddenly, because of a queer way she had of squinting one eye when she looked at me, it came to me.

"She was the wife of one of my gallant Fusiliers!

"I forgot all about my determination not to sing and burst out with 'The Midget Mascot' song.

"Aunt Rosie was so astonished to hear me sing that all she could say was:

" 'Why, good gracious! My birdie is singing!'

" 'Of course she's singing!' declared the woman. 'She's one of the finest songstresses in the country!'

" 'How do you know that?' asked Aunt Rosie looking very puzzled indeed.

" 'Because this is the same bird that belonged to my husband's regiment,' replied the woman. 'He told me before he went off to India that she'd disappeared during the mine riots and that no one had seen her again. Naturally the whole regiment assumed she'd been killed . . . I do declare!' she muttered. 'This is the strangest thing I've ever seen.'

"By this time Aunt Rosie was as excited as the woman was.

" 'Are you sure it's the same one?' she asked. 'You know, I found him working in a miserable coal mine. It cost me twelve guineas to get that miner fellow to give him up.'

" 'He's not a he,' the woman said, laughing. 'He's a she! And her name is Pippinella!'

" 'Pippinella!' cried Aunt Rosie. 'What a beautiful name. But if it's a hen how is it that she sings? I always understood hens couldn't sing.'

" 'Nonsense!' declared the woman. 'Hens sing just as well as cocks. Especially this one.'

"Well," Pippinella continued, "I was glad at last to be identified. For a long time now I had been called Dick or Birdie—or just simply 'it.' But, of course, now I had to worry about Aunt Rosie discovering I could sing. How would I ever make her understand that I wanted a companion of my own kind?

"But it came about quite simply. I suppose I must have gotten to look rather sad and mopey after a while. It wasn't intentional, but the old lady noticed it. For one day, when she took the cover off my cage and gave me seed and water, I was delighted to hear her say:

" 'Dear, dear, tut-tut-tut! How sad we look this morning. Maybe my little Pippinella wants a mate. Yes? All right. Aunt Rosie will go and get her another little birdie to talk to!'

"Then she put on her bonnet and went off to the animal shop to get me a husband. Well, I wish you could have seen the husband she brought back."

Pippinella closed her eyes and shrugged up the shoulders of her wings.

"He was a fool—a perfect fool. I've never seen such a stupid bird in my life. The old lady supplied us with cotton wool and other stuffs to build a nest with. Now building a nest in a cage is a very simple matter, provided the cage is big enough. And ours was amply large. My new husband—his name was Twink—said he knew all about it. We set to work. He didn't agree with anything I did, and I didn't agree with anything he did. And then he'd argue with me—my goodness, how he argued! Just as though he knew, you know! First it was about the position of the nest. I'd get it half done in one corner of the cage, and then he'd put his empty head on one side and say, 'No, my dear, I don't think that's a good place. The light will shine too much in the children's eyes. Let's put it over in this corner.'

"And he'd want to pull it all down and rebuild it on the other side of the cage. And the next time it would be the way the inside was lined. Even when I was sitting in the nest he'd come fussing around, pulling bits out here and there—right from under me.

"Finally I saw that if I was ever going to get a brood raised at all that year I had better just rule him out of the building altogether. Then we had a violent row, during which he pecked me on the head and I knocked him off the perch. But I won my point. I told him that if he touched the nest again I wouldn't lay a single egg.

"But one thing must be said for Twink. And that was that he had a marvelous voice."

"Better than your own?" asked the Doctor.

"Oh, by far," said Pippinella. "In the upper register— well, it almost seemed at times as if there weren't any note he couldn't reach. And even in the bass his tones were wonderfully clear and full. Of course, like all husbands, he didn't care to have his wife sing. But as a matter of fact, I never attempted to compete with him because when eggs and youngsters have to be looked after, we women don't get much time for it.

"There was great excitement the day when our family at last appeared. They were five strong, healthy birds. Aunt Rosie was even more thrilled and worked up than we were. Ten times a day she would come to the nest and peer in; and every group of her friends who visited her would also be brought to have a look. And they all said the same things: 'Oh, my, aren't they ugly!' Goodness! I don't know what they expected newborn birds to look like, I'm sure. Maybe they thought they ought to be hatched out with bonnets and capes on.

"It was now that the real work began for me and my husband. Feeding five hungry children is a big job—even when there are two of you at it. Aunt Rosie used to bring us chopped egg and cracker crumbs six times a day. Each lot lasted only about an hour and a quarter, for we had to

"Ten times a day she would come and peer in"

shovel it into those hungry mouths every thirty minutes. And then there was the lettuce and apple and other green stuff that had to be given them as well.

"But it was lots of fun, even if it was hard work. Twink, I found, after the nest-building problems were over, was not nearly so stupid and irritating. We got along very well together. He used to sit on the edge of the nest and sing to me when I was keeping the children warm between meals, and many were the beautiful lullabies he made up.

"When the brood was strong enough to leave the nest we both felt awfully proud with the five hulking youngsters crowding on the perch, all in a row beside us. Of course they quarreled, the way children will, and the two biggest tried to bully the rest. Twink and I had our hands full keeping them in order, I can tell you. With seven full-grown birds in it, the cage was now none too big.

"Well, the day came when Aunt Rosie decided she would have to part with some of the family. Many of her friends wanted canaries, and one by one my children went off to new homes, till finally only Twink and I were left. And then because one of her friends had told the old lady that cocks sing better if they are alone (which is perfectly true) she gave Twink a separate cage and put him in another room.

"So toward the end of the summer I found myself alone again. A swallow had built her nest under the eaves of the roof, just above my window. During the summer I had watched her hatch out two broods and teach them to fly. Now I saw her with many of her friends, gathering and chattering and skimming around the house. They were getting ready to fly south to avoid the cold of the coming winter. I wondered what adventures and strange things they would see on their long trip. And once more I had a vague sort of hankering for a free life that would let me wander where I would.

"For a whole day the swallows kept gathering, more and more arriving all the time. I could hear them twittering, making no end of noise, and the top of the streetlamp was just covered with them. Seeing them made me feel like traveling, the way people going off always does.

"At last, with a great farewell fluttering and whistling, they took to the air and set off on their journey. I felt rather sad in the silence that they left behind. But presently through the window I saw Aunt Rosie's white Persian cat slinking along the street with a bird in her mouth. And once more I was reminded of the security and comfort I enjoyed as a cage bird; once more I consoled myself, as the old man came and lit the lamp, that a quiet, stay-at-home, regular life had its compensations. Who knows whether, if Twink and I had built our nest in some forest or hedgerow, instead of raising our brood to fine healthy growth, we would have seen our children carried off before our very eyes by some prowling cat?"

· The Ninth Chapter ·
THE OLD WINDMILL

I HAVE told you that I made several rather odd friends while I was at Aunt Rosie's house," Pippinella continued. "Among them was a window cleaner. The old lady was frightfully particular about having her windows cleaned, and she had a regular cleaner come, a man who made a business of cleaning windows.

"He was the funniest person to look at I have ever seen— one of those faces that makes you smile the moment you catch sight of it. He whistled cheerful tunes all the time while he was working. He had a very big mouth and when he breathed on the glass to put an extra shine on it I always had to laugh outright. I used to look forward to his coming no end. And he took a great liking to me. He always spent an especially long time over my window, getting it immaculately clean with his red and white polishing cloth. And he'd whistle and make faces at me through the glass, and I'd whistle back to him. I often thought it would be lots of fun to have him for an owner. I was sure he'd be much more interesting than Aunt Rosie.

"I always felt dreadfully sorry when he was gone. And I would spatter my bath water all over the window with my

"He'd whistle and make faces at me through the glass"

wings, so as to make it nice and dirty. I knew that Aunt Rosie had lots of money to pay for cleaning windows. So I made it necessary for him to come once a week instead of once a month.

"One day Aunt Rosie was speaking to him in my room while he was doing the inside of the window, and their conversation turned to the subject of canaries. He had made some very flattering remarks about me and, to my great joy, she asked him if he would like to have me. Now that she had another bird who sang all day, the novelty had worn off and she did not mind giving me away.

"Then my dirtying up of the windows every week may have had something to do with her willingness to part with me—she was one of those frightfully particular housekeepers. But so long as I was to go to the window cleaner, I was just as well pleased.

"Well, my friend was quite overcome with joy when the old lady told him he could have me. And that night he wrapped me up and took me to his home.

"It was the strangest place. He lived in an old windmill. It had not worked in many years and was a kind of a ruin. I imagine he got it very cheap—if indeed he paid anything at all for rent of it. But inside he had made it very comfortable. It was just a round tower, like most windmills, but of good, solid stonework. He lived in a little room at the bottom, which he had furnished with homemade chairs and tables and shelves. It had a little stove, whose pipe ran up the tower and out at the top. He had no family—lived all by himself and cooked his own meals. He had lots and lots of secondhand books, which he bought after the covers had fallen off them—very cheaply, I suppose.

"He spent all his evenings reading and writing. I believe he was secretly writing a book himself, because he carefully kept all the sheets of paper he wrote on in a tin box in a hole in the floor. He was quite a character, but one of the nicest men I ever knew. He cleaned windows only because he needed money to live on. Of that I am sure. Because the windows of his own home were in a shocking state, so he evidently didn't polish glass for the love of it.

"And so I settled down to live with my funny new master. He was indeed an odd fellow. I believe if he had been able he would have spent all his time reading and writing. But he had to go to work in the morning and he was gone until teatime. I used to look forward to Sunday because then he was home all day. The rest of the week I felt rather lonely. When he left in the morning he locked up his old windmill with a homemade lock, and all day long I had nothing to do but watch the rats chase one another over his homemade furniture or look at the view through the window cleaner's dirty window.

"But the evenings were great fun. When he came back home my friend would talk to me the whole time he was cooking his dinner. Of course, he had no idea I understood him. But I think he was glad of anyone to converse with. For he, too, led a very lonely life—and what is more, unlike me he was not used to it. Yes, he'd tell me the whole day's doings while he fried his eggs or stirred his soup—what houses he had been in, what sort of people he had seen, whether their windows were extra dirty, and if they had birdcages hanging in them or not. In this way he often brought me news of Aunt Rosie and my husband, Twink, and even of my children, who had gone to other houses whose windows he was accustomed to clean.

"I was puzzled about my strange friend a good deal—about what had been his life before he took to this profession. He was a man cut off, as it were, from all his fellows. I often wondered whether he had some secret that made it necessary for him to live thus—almost in hiding, as you might say.

"Well, the winter wore pleasantly on, and soon the spring was at hand once more. This was a time when my master was particularly busy, for everybody was doing spring cleaning—which always means a lot of extra window washing. Some nights he did not get home till quite late. When the days got warmer he would put my cage outside on the wall. And one day he left me in the open air when he went to work in the morning.

"He would tell me the day's doings while he stirred his soup"

" 'It's a pleasant day, Pip,' said he. 'And I don't see why you should be shut up just because I'm not here. I'll be back early—to lunch. It's Saturday and I mean to take a half holiday, no matter how many housekeepers want their windows cleaned.'

"Then he took me up to the top of the mill tower, where there was an old, leaky, ramshackle room, which was never used. And he hung my cage outside the window on a nail. It was a difficult sort of place to get to because there wasn't any stair—just poles and ladders and things to scramble up by.

" 'There you are, Pip,' said he. 'You'll be quite safe here. It's a sort of breaknecky place, but no worse than some of the window ledges I have to stand on at my job. I've put you here so you'll be safe from the cats while I'm away. So long.'

"Then he made his way down the tower again and I watched him come out of the door below and walk briskly away toward the town.

"It was very nice to be in the open. It was the first time my cage had been set out this year. The mild spring sunshine was invigorating and refreshing. From my lofty lookout I watched wild birds of various kinds flying here and there and everywhere.

"Lunchtime came, but my friend did not return.

"Oh, well, I thought, he has been delayed. He can't afford to disappoint his customers. Some old lady has asked him to stay on and do a few extra windows. He'll turn up soon.

"And even when teatime came and still he hadn't appeared, I continued to make excuses for him. But when the sun had set and the evening star was twinkling in the dusky sky and my cage had not yet been taken in, I began to get really anxious.

"As the darkness settled down about my cage I began to shiver with the cold. It was still, you see, quite early in the year, and even indoors I was accustomed to have a cover over me.

"I got no sleep at all. All night I kept wondering what could have become of my friend. Had he fallen from some high place while cleaning windows? Had he been run over? Something must have happened to him, that was certain. Because he was always very thoughtful of me and he couldn't have forgotten that he had left me out in the open.

And even supposing that that had slipped his memory, he could never have forgotten that I would need food and fresh water by the end of the day.

"Well, the dawn came at last—after a night that seemed a whole eternity in length. As the sun gradually rose in the heavens and the warmth of it glowed upon my shivering wings my spirits revived somewhat. There was still a little seed left in my trough and some water in the pot. I was about to take breakfast—which I always did at sunrise— when it suddenly occurred to me that I had better econo- mize and make my supply last as long as possible. Because the more I thought of it the more certain I became that I had seen the last of my good friend the window cleaner.

"You see, with an ordinary person who had a family liv- ing with him or friends calling at his house or tradesmen delivering daily goods, I would sooner or later have re- ceived assistance. But this man never had a soul come near him from one end of the year to the other. So I made up my mind to two things: first, something serious had happened to my owner; second, that I need expect no help or food except by some chance accident. It was a bad out- look all around.

"Still where there's life there's hope. I ate a very tiny breakfast—just enough to keep me going. Lunchtime came and I did the same—and the same again at dusk. Another cold, miserable night. Another shivering dawn. By now I had only a few grains of food left. My spirits were dread- fully low. I ate the last of my supply and, utterly worn out, fell asleep as the sun began to rise.

"Just how long I slept I don't know—till an hour or so beyond noon, I imagine. I was awakened by a great racket, and, opening my eyes, found the sky dark with rain clouds. A storm was brewing. Every few seconds great tongues of

"Great tongues of lightning flashed across the face of the heavens"

lightning flashed across the face of the gloomy heavens, followed by deafening crashes of thunder.

"As the first big drops of rain came plopping into the floor of my cage I saw I was in for a good soaking, in addition to my other troubles. But that storm was a blessing in disguise. Such a storm! I have never seen anything like it. My mill tower, placed where all the winds of heaven could reach it, got the full benefit of its fury. Five minutes after I woke up I was drenched and chilled to the marrow of my bones. I tried to crouch down under my water pot and get some shelter that way. But it was no use. The gale blew the rain in every direction, and there was no escaping it. The floor of my cage was just swimming in water.

"Suddenly I heard a rending, crackling sound and saw a piece of mill roof hurtle earthward through the air, just wrenched off the tower by the strength of the wind. In between the claps of thunder I heard other crashes below me. All sorts of things were being blown down or smashed by the tempest.

"And then, *zip!* I felt my cage struck upward, as though someone had hit the bottom with the palm of his hand. And the next minute I, too, was sailing earthward. My cage had been blown off its nail.

"After my cage jumped off its nail and started sailing through the air I haven't a very clear recollection of things. I remember feeling it turn over and over till I was giddy, and on its way down I think it struck a roof or something and bounced off. I clung to the perch with my claws— more out of fright than anything else—and just turned over with it as it spun.

"Then there was a crash. Suddenly I found myself sitting in a puddle on the ground, quite unharmed but very wet. The two halves of my cage, neatly broken in the center, lay on either side of me. The rain was still beating down in torrents. I had landed on a cobble pavement, right in front of the mill. Under the steps there was a hole between the stones. I crept into the shelter of it and tried to collect my scattered wits while I waited for the rain to stop.

"So, I thought to myself, I am a free bird at last! If this storm hadn't come along and blown my cage down I would have starved to death up there in two or three more days, at most. Well, well! And now, after wondering so

often what it would feel like to be uncaged, here I am—
free! But, oh, so hungry, so cold and so wet!

"And thus—"

"But what happened to the window cleaner?" Gub-Gub
interrupted. "Why hadn't he come back?"

"Wait and you will see," said Pippinella severely.

"And thus began still another chapter of my story—
when, after being born and brought up a cage bird I was
suddenly made by Fate, willy-nilly, into a wild one. For the
present, sad and unhappy though I was about my good
friend the window cleaner, I only had two ideas in my
mind—to get dry and to find food. I was literally starving."

PART TWO

· The First Chapter ·

THE GREEN CANARY
LEARNS TO FLY

AFTER about half an hour the storm abated. The rain stopped and the sun came out. I at once left my rat hole and started to fly around in the open to get the wet shaken out of my feathers.

"I was astonished to discover that I could hardly fly at all. I decided that this was due to the soaking I had had—and to exhaustion from want of food. But even when, by constant fluttering, I got perfectly dry I found that the best I could do was just tiny, short distances; and that the effort of these was frightfully tiring. As a cage bird I had learned to keep up a flight only from one perch to another—hardly flying at all, you might say. Before I could take to the air like a regular free bird, I had to learn—just as though I were a baby leaving the nest for the first time.

"Well, there was no food around here. And if I was to go foraging for any I had better get busy. So I set to work practicing my flight. There was an old packing case close to the door of the mill and I began by flying up on to it and down again. Presently while I was doing this I noticed a lean, hungry-looking cat watching me. Ha, ha, my beauty,

"Presently I noticed a cat watching me"

I thought. I may be a very green cage bird, but I know you
and your kind.

"And by short stages I flew up on the roofs of some old
tumbledown outhouses that stood near. She followed me
up there. Then I returned to the yard. In spite of my poor
flying I could keep out of her claws so long as I knew
where she was. And I never lingered anywhere in the
neighborhood of an ambushing place, where she could
pounce out on me unawares.

"In the meantime I kept on practicing. And although it was dreadfully exhausting work, I felt I was improving hourly and would soon be able to make the top of the mill tower on one flight. From there I hoped I would be able to get inside the building through a hole in the roof and make my way down to the kitchen, where I could find some food.

"Seeing what a poor flyer I was, Mme. Pussy, in the mean-souled way that cats have, had made up her mind that I was injured or a weakling and would be easy prey. And she stayed around and watched and waited. She was determined she'd get me. But I was equally determined that she wouldn't.

"Most people would think it a simple matter for a cage bird to change herself into a wild one. But wild birds are educated very young to take care of themselves. They learn from their parents and other birds where to search for water, at what seasons seed is to be found, where and when to look for certain kinds of berries, what places to roost in at night so they'll be protected from winds and safe from pouncing weasels, and—well, a million and a half other things. All this education I had missed.

"Well," Pippinella continued, "I saw that if I was to survive in the open I would have to be very careful and take no risks. That was the chief reason that I began by making my way into the inside of the building. Within its walls I should be safe. I knew that owls and hawks and shrikes swept around this hill every once in a while on the lookout for anything small enough to kill. And until my flying was a great deal better I would stand no earthly chance of escape, once a bird of prey started out to get me.

"I found a hole in the top of the tower, and I made my way downward through all sorts of funny dark flues and passages till I came to the kitchen door. This was locked.

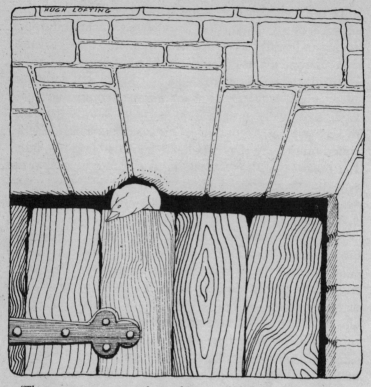

"There was a space over the top big enough for me to slip through"

But luckily the old thing was all warped and it didn't fit very well. There was a space over the top big enough for me to slip through.

"I lived in that kitchen for a week. I found my seed where I knew the window cleaner always kept it, in a paper bag on the mantelshelf. In the corner by the stove there was a bucket of water. So I was well stocked with provisions, besides being snugly protected behind solid stone walls from my natural enemies and the cold of the nights. There I went on practicing my flying. Round and round that kitchen I flew, counting the number of laps. And after I had got as high as a thousand I thought, Well, I don't know just how far that would be in a straight line, but it must be a good long way.

"Still I wasn't satisfied. I knew that often in the open I would have to fly miles and miles at high speed. And I kept on circling the kitchen by the hour. One morning, when I rested on the mantelpiece after two hours of steady flying, I suddenly spied that wretched cat, squatting behind the stove, watching me. How she had gotten in I don't know—certainly not the way I had come. But cats are mysterious creatures and can slip through unbelievably small spaces when they want to.

"Well, anyway, there she was. My comfortable kitchen wasn't safe anymore. However, I found a place to rest nights—the funniest roosting place you ever saw—on a string of dried onions that hung from the ceiling. I knew she couldn't reach me there, and I could go to sleep in safety.

"But as a matter of fact, I got very little rest. That cat was on my mind all the time. And although I knew perfectly well that she couldn't jump as high as that string, somehow —they're such horribly clever things—every time she moved I woke up, thinking maybe she'd discovered some devilish trick to reach me by, after all.

"Finally I said to myself, Tomorrow I will leave the mill and take to the open. It's a little earlier than I had planned to go, but I'll get no peace, now that she has found her way here. Tomorrow I will journey forth to seek my fortune.

"Back I traveled through the little space above the door, up the dark, dusty, dilapidated mill tower, until I came to the hole in the stonework at the top. It was a beautiful morning. A lovely scene lay before me as I—"

"But when's the window cleaner coming back?" whined Gub-Gub. "I want to know what happened to that window cleaner."

"Be patient," said the Doctor. "Pippinella has told you to wait and see."

"A lovely scene," the canary repeated, "lay before me as I gazed out over the countryside. For a moment I felt almost scared to launch myself down upon the bosom of the air from that height. I picked out a little copse over to the eastward. That can't be more than a quarter of a mile away, I said to myself. I can surely fly that far. All right—here goes!

"And I shot off the tower top in the direction of the little wood. And now once more I found myself faced with the problems of my own inexperience. I had never before flown high up in the open air. I had no idea of how to tackle the winds and the air currents that pushed me and turned me this way and that. Any ordinary bird would have made that copse with hardly a flutter—just sailed down to it with motionless, outstretched wings. But I— well, I was like some badly loaded boat without a rudder in a gale. I pitched and tossed and wobbled and staggered. I heard some crows who passed laughing at me in their hoarse, cracky voices.

" 'Haw, haw!' they crackled. 'Look at the feather duster the wind blew up! Put your tail down, chicken! Stick to it! Mind you don't fall! Whoa!'

"They're vulgar, low birds, crows. But I suppose I must have looked comical enough, flustering and flapping around at the mercy of the fitful wind. I got down to the woods somehow and made a sort of wild spread-eagle landing in the top boughs of an oak. I was all exhausted. But I felt encouraged, anyway. I had proved that I could get where I wanted to, even with a moderate wind against me.

"I rested a while to regain my breath and then started hopping around through the woods. I found it much easier to get my wings all snarled up in the blackberry brambles than to shoot in and out of the thickets like the other birds did. But I took the crows' advice and stuck to it, knowing that the only way to learn even this was by practice.

"While I was hopping around, making discoveries and collecting experiences, I became aware that once more I was being watched by enemies. This time it was a large sparrow hawk. Whenever I came out into a clearing I'd see the same round-shouldered bird, sitting motionless at the top of some tall tree. He pretended to be dozing in the sun. But I felt pretty certain that he had noticed my awkward, clumsy flight and was only waiting for a chance to swoop on me. I knew that so long as I stayed near the bramble thickets I was fairly safe. For with his wide wings he couldn't possibly follow me into the little tiny spaces of the thorny blackberry tangles.

"After a while I supposed he had given me up as a bad job. For he flew off with easy, gliding flight and made away over the treetops as though leaving the woods for good. Then, feeling safe once more, I proceeded with further explorations and after a little I decided to venture out in the open again.

"This time I thought I'd try traveling downwind. And I set out flying back in the general direction from which I had approached the wood. It was much easier work, but required quite a lot of skill to keep a straight line with the wind at my back.

"About halfway across the fields that lay beneath the copse and the windmill hill I noticed a flock of sparrows rise out of a hedge below me in a great state of alarm. They were looking upward at the sky as they scattered, chattering, in all directions. They were evidently in a panic about something. And suddenly I guessed what it was—I had forgotten all about the hawk. I turned my head and there he was, not more than a hundred and fifty yards behind, speeding after me like a bullet. I never had such a fright in my life. There was no place in the fields where I could hide.

"The hole in the tower, I thought to myself. If I can reach that I am safe. He isn't small enough to follow me into that hole in the roof.

"And putting on the best speed I could, I shut my beak tight and made for the old mill.

"It was a terrible race," Pippinella went on, shaking her head. "That hawk had the speed of the wind itself, and there were times when I thought I'd never get away from him. I was afraid to look back, lest even the turning of my head delay my flight. I could hear the *swish, swish, swish* of his great wings beating the air behind me.

"But fortunately the rising sparrows had warned me in time to get a pretty fair start on him. And in so short a flight even he was not swift enough to overtake me. He came awfully close to it, though. As I shot into the mill roof and tumbled down gasping for breath among the cobwebs, I saw his great shadow sweep over the hole not more than a foot behind me.

" 'You wait!' I heard him hiss as he tilted upward and veered away over the mill roof. 'I'll get you yet!' "

"You haven't forgotten about the window cleaner, have you?" asked Gub-Gub. "What's happening to him all this time?"

"Oh, be quiet," snapped Jip.

"I spent the night in the tower," Pippinella continued. "The cat did not know I was there yet, so I wasn't bothered by her. But I felt very miserable as I settled down to sleep. An ordinary free bird, I suppose, would not have been greatly disturbed by being chased by a hawk—so long as he got away. But it was my first experience in the wild. And it seemed to me as though the whole world were full of enemies, of creatures that wanted to kill me. I felt dreadfully friendless and lonely.

"After a fitful, nightmarish sort of sleep I was awakened in the morning by a very agreeable sound, the love song of a greenfinch. Somewhere on a ledge just outside the hole a bird was singing. And he was singing to me. I was, as it were, being serenaded at my window. I got up, brushed the cobwebs out of my tail, spruced up my feathers, and prepared to go out and take a look at my caller.

"I peeped cautiously through the hole and there he was —the handsomest little cock you ever saw in your life. His head was thrown back, his wings slightly raised, and his throat puffed out. He was singing away with all his might. I do not know any song myself that I like better than the love song of the greenfinch in the spring. There's a peculiar dreamy, poetic sort of quality to it that no other bird melody possesses. You have no idea what it did for me that morning. In a moment I had forgotten about the hawk and the cat and all my troubles. The whole world seemed changed, friendly, full of pleasant adventure. I waited there, listening in the dark, till he had finished. Then I stepped out of the hole onto the roof.

" 'Good morning,' he said, smiling in an embarrassed sort of way. 'I hope I didn't wake you too early.'

" 'Oh, not at all,' I answered. 'It was very good of you to come!'

" 'Well,' he said, 'I saw you being chased by that beastly old sparrow hawk last night. I had noticed you in the copse earlier. From your sort of stiff way of flying I guessed you were a cage bird just newly freed. I'm glad you got away from the old brute. I was awfully afraid you wouldn't. You are partly a greenfinch yourself, are you not?'

" 'Yes,' I replied. 'My mother was a greenfinch and my father a canary.'

" 'I guessed that too, from your feathers,' said he. 'I think you're very pretty—with those fine yellow bars in your wings.

" 'Would you care to take a fly around the woods?' my new acquaintance asked me. 'It's a pleasant morning.'

" 'Thank you,' I said. 'I certainly would. I'm very hungry and I don't know very much as yet about foraging for food in the open.'

" 'Well, let's be off, then,' he said. 'Wait till I take a look around to make sure the squint-eyed old hawk isn't browsing about. Then we'll go across to Eastdale Farm. I know a granary there where there are whole sacks of millet seed kept. And some of it is always lying around loose near the door where the men load it in. Ha, the coast is clear! Come along.'

"So off we went, as happy as you please—for all the world like two children out for a romp. On the way my friend, whose name I found was Nippit, gave me no end of new tips about flying—how to set the wings against a twisting air current, what effect had the spreading of the tail fanlike when the wind was behind me, dodges for raising myself without the work of flapping, how to drop or dive without turning over.

"We reached the farm he had spoken of. A fine, substantial, old-fashioned place, it looked just charming in early morning sunlight.

" 'I don't think the men are up yet,' he said '—not that they would bother us even if they were. But it's more comfortable getting your breakfast without disturbances.

There's the granary, that big brick building with the elms hanging over it.'

"He led me to the door at the back, and there, as he had said, was quite a lot of millet seed scattered around loose, where it had fallen from the sacks on their way into the storerooms.

"While we were gobbling away he suddenly shouted, 'Look out!' at the top of his voice. And we both leapt into the air in the nick of time. The farm dog, one of those spaniels they use for shooting, had made a rush at us from behind. I hadn't seen him coming at all. But my friend's eyes were twice as sharp as mine, and he never ate near the ground without keeping one eye constantly on the lookout all around. His vigilance had saved my life."

· The Second Chapter ·
NIPPIT, THE GREENFINCH

NIPPIT and I became closer friends than ever, and I often think that if it had not been for him I would never have survived the life of the open or be here now to tell the tale. His experience not only protected me from my enemies, but his wisdom provided me with food. He took me under his care, as it were, and with great patience he taught me the things a wild bird needs to know."

To the animals' great surprise, Pippinella, who had always seemed a very practical sort of bird, at this point, sniffed slightly, as though for the moment overcome with emotion.

"You must excuse me," she gulped. "I know it's very silly of me, but whenever I think of Nippit I nearly always get sort of sentimental and wobbly in the voice—I mean when I think about the part I am now going to tell you. . . . I was terribly fond of him—more fond than I have ever been of anyone or anything. And he was most frightfully in love with me. One moonlight night we swore to be true to each other till death, to go off and find a place to build a nest and raise a family of young ones. We described to

each other what the place should look like. We were †
bly particular about the details. It was a real romance.

"Next day we started off. We journeyed a great distance.
And finally we came to the seashore. We explored a little
bay—the very loveliest thing you could wish to see. Big
drooping willows hung down off rocks and dabbled their
wands in the blue water. Beautiful wild flowers and
colored mosses carpeted the shore. It was a secluded little
cove where people never came. The peace and the beauty
of it were just ideal. And there at the bottom of the bay,
where a little sparkly mountain stream fell laughing into
the sea, we found the spot we had come so far to seek—
exact in every detail."

"Maybe the window cleaner sprained his ankle," murmured Gub-Gub, "or ate something that disagreed with
him and had to go to a hospital. But I would like to know
why he didn't send someone to take his canary in."

"For heaven's sake, will you wait?" growled Jip. "Keep
quiet! Wait and see what happened!"

"But I don't like waiting," said Gub-Gub. "I never was a
good waiter. Why doesn't she come right out with it? She
knows what happened to her friend."

"Gub-Gub," said the Doctor wearily, "if you don't keep
quiet you will have to leave the wagon."

"Right away," Pippinella continued, "we set to work
hunting for materials to build a nest. You know, each kind
of bird has fads and fancies about nest-building—each one
uses materials of his own special kind. The greenfinch's
nest is not more extraordinary in this than any others; but
some of the stuffs used are not always easily found. In
these parts they were exceptionally scarce. So we went off
hunting in different directions, agreeing that either should
come and let the other know as soon as the stuff we were
after was discovered.

"I went a long way down the shore and after about an hour's search I came upon the material we sought. It was a special kind of dry grass. I marked the spot in my mind and set off to tell my mate. I had some difficulty in finding him, but eventually I did—and" (again Pippinella's voice grew tearful) "he was talking to a greenfinch hen. She was very handsome, slightly younger than either Nippit or myself. The instant I saw them talking together, something told me the end of our romance had come.

"He introduced me to her—rather awkwardly. And she smirked and smiled like the brazen hussy that she was. It was now too late in the evening to go on with the nest-building; and anyway, I had no heart for it. After we had had something to eat and taken a drink in the little sparkling stream we all three roosted on a flowering hawthorn bush.

"I cannot believe that it was all Nippit's fault. But by morning I knew what I must do. Quietly, while my faithless mate and that hypocritical minx still slept, I dropped to a lower branch of the hawthorn bush and made my way down to the edge of the sea."

As Pippinella paused a moment in her story, evidently very close to the verge of tears, the Doctor was glad of an interruption that arrived just at the right moment to cover her embarrassment. It was the chief tent rigger, who wished to consult Manager Dolittle about buying a new tent for the snakes. The old one, he said, was so full of mends and patches that he felt it would be better economy to throw it away and buy a new one.

When the discussion was over and the tent rigger had departed, Pippinella took a sip of water and presently went on with her story.

"The day was rising in the east. The calm water reflected the mingled gray and pink of the dawn sky, and away out on the horizon little flashes of gold here and there showed where the sun would soon come up.

"It was a lovely scene. But I didn't care. I hated everything about this place now; the snug bay, the weeping willows, the murmuring mountain brook—everything.

"Some birds nearby started their morning song. A finch flew past and twittered a greeting to me on the wing. But still I sat on there, gazing out from the sands toward the wide-stretching sea. It seemed to yawn and roll lazily, rubbing the sleep out of its eyes as the night retired from the face of the waters and the rising sun glowed around its rim. Its mystery, its vastness, called to me, sympathizing with my mood.

" 'The sea!' I murmured. 'I've never crossed the salt water. I've never looked on foreign lands, as all the other wild birds have. Those jungles my mother told me of, where blue and yellow macaws climb on crimson flowering vines —they must be nice; they would be new. There surely, among fresh scenes and different company, I shall be able to forget. Everything around me here I hate, for it reminds me of my mate who was false, of my love that was spurned.'

"You see, it was my first romance, so I felt especially sentimental. 'Very well,' I said, 'I will leave this land and cross the sea.'

"I went down closer to the breaking surf and stood upon the firm, smooth, hard-packed sand of the beach. I noticed a small bird, a goldfinch, coming inland. He looked as though he had flown a long way. I hailed him.

" 'What country,' I asked, 'lies beyond this ocean?'

"With a neat curve he landed on the sand beside me. I noticed him eyeing my crossbred feathers with curiosity.

" 'Many lands,' he answered. 'Where do you want to go?'

" 'What country,' I asked, 'lies beyond the ocean?' "

" 'Anywhere,' I answered. 'Anywhere, so long as I get away from here.'

" 'That's odd,' said he. 'Most birds are coming this way now. Spring and summer are the seasons here. I came over with the goldfinches. The main flock arrived last night. But I was delayed and followed on behind. Did you ever cross the ocean before? Do you know the way?'

" 'No,' I said, bursting into tears. 'I know no geography or navigation. I'm a cage bird. My heart is broken. I want to reach the land where the blue and yellow macaws climb ropes of crimson orchids.'

" 'Well,' said he, 'that could be almost anywhere in the tropics. But it's pretty dangerous, you know, ocean travel, if you're not experienced at it.'

" 'I don't care anything about the danger,' I cried. 'I'm desperate. I want to go to a new land and begin life all over again. Good-bye!'

"And springing into the air I headed out over the sea just as the full glory of the rising sun flooded the blue waters in dazzling light."

· The Third Chapter ·
EBONY ISLAND

JOHN DOLITTLE stared at Pippinella in amazement.

"That was an extremely dangerous thing for you to have undertaken," he said. "I'm surprised you are here at all to tell the story."

"Well, if I hadn't been sort of desperate with grief I would never have embarked upon such a mad piece of craziness. It was only after I had flown steadily for two hours that I fully realized what I had done. On all sides, north, east, south, and west, the sky met the sea in a flat ring. No clouds marred the even color of the heavens; nothing broke the smoothness of the blue-green sea. In turning my head to look back I had changed my direction without thinking. Now I didn't even know if I was going the same way or not. I tried to remember from what quarter the wind had been blowing when I started. But I couldn't recollect. And anyway there was no wind blowing now. So I could get no guidance from that.

"A terrible feeling of helplessness came over me as I gazed down—I was flying at a great height—at the wide-stretching water below me. Where was I? Whither was I going?

"And then it occurred to me that in this, as in my other first difficulties of freedom, I had got to learn—to learn or perish. Well, I thought, I'll go and take a closer look at the surface of the water. I'm too high up to see anything here. Maybe I can learn something.

"So I shut my wings and dropped a couple of thousand feet. As I came nearer to the water I noticed many little patches of brown on it, thousands of them. They were evidently some kind of seaweed or grass. They floated in sort of straggly chains, like long processions of tortoises or crabs. But these chains all lay in the same direction.

" 'Ah-hah!' I said. 'That's a current.' I had seen something of the same kind before, grasses and leaves pushed across a lake by a river that flowed into it. And I knew there was a force in that water down below me that drove all those weed clumps the same way.

"I'll follow the drift of that weed, I thought. It will anyhow keep me in a straight line and maybe bring me to the mouth of the river from which the current flows.

"Well, my idea would have been all right if my strength had held out. You must remember that it wasn't many months since I had flown at all in the open. And suddenly as I skimmed over the weed chains I got an awful cramp in my left wing muscle. I felt I just simply had to stop and rest. But where? I couldn't sit on the water like a duck. There was nothing for it but to keep on. I had been going three hours at seventy miles an hour, some two hundred miles—by far the longest flight I had ever made. The wonder was that I hadn't given out before.

"Things looked bad. In spite of all my efforts to keep at the same level I was coming down nearer the water all the time. Finally I was skimming along only a few feet above the swells. I was so near now I could see the tiny sea beetles clinging to the weed tufts. In between, in the clear spaces, I saw my own reflection looking up at me, a tiny fool of a land bird with wildly flapping outstretched wings, trying to make her way across a never-ending ocean, lost, giving out, coming nearer to a watery grave second by second.

"The thing that saved me was the little sea beetles that crawled upon the floating weed. They gave me an idea. If the shred of weed could carry them, I thought, why wouldn't larger clumps of it carry me? I looked along the straggling chains that wound over the sea ahead of me. About a hundred yards farther on I spied a bigger bunch of the stuff. Making a tremendous effort, I spurted along and just gained it in time. I dropped on it as lightly as I could in the exhausted condition I had reached. To my great delight it bore me up—for the moment. The relief of being able to relax my weary muscles and rest was just wonderful. And for the present I didn't bother about anything else, but just stood there on my little seaweed boat and rose and fell on the heaving bosom of the sea.

"But soon I noticed that my feet were getting wet. The water had risen right over my ankles. My odd craft would carry my small weight for a few moments only; then it had gone slowly under. It was of the utmost importance that I should not, in my exhausted state, get my feathers waterlogged. I looked around. Not more than six feet away another clump of weed was floating, about the size of a tea tray. With a spring and a flip I leapt from my old raft to the new one. Being a little larger, it carried me a moment or two longer than the one I had left. But it, too, sank in time and the warning water rising around my feet drove me on to yet another refuge.

"It wasn't the most comfortable way in the world to take a rest—hopping from one sinking island to another. Still, it was miles better than nothing. In the short jumps I did not have to use my wings much and I already felt the cramp in my left shoulder improving. I decided that I could keep this up as long as I liked. It was the steady drive of constant flying that tired me. So long as there were large weed clumps enough and no storms came, I was safe.

"But that was all. I wasn't going ahead. The current was moving very slowly—and that in the wrong direction for me. I was hungry and thirsty. There was no food here, and no prospect of getting any. There were, it is true, the tiny sea creatures that crawled upon the weed. But I was afraid to eat them, saturated in salt water, lest the thirst I had already should grow worse. The only thing to do for the present was to be thankful for this assistance, to rest up, and then to go on again.

"Presently I began to notice the sun. It had been getting higher and higher all the time since I had left land, but soon it seemed to be standing still and then to descend. That meant that midday had been passed. I began to wonder if I could get much farther before night fell. There was no moon, I knew, till early morning, and in the darkness flying for me would be impossible if I could not see my guiding current.

"While I was wondering I suddenly spied a flock of birds coming toward me in the opposite direction to my own. They were evidently land birds, and when they got nearer I saw that they were finches, though of a kind that I had never seen before. They were slamming along at a great pace and their freshness and speed made me feel very foolish and weak, squatting on my lump of seaweed like a turtle. It occurred to me that this was a chance to get some advice that might not come again in a long while. So, putting my best foot forward, as you might say, I flew up to meet them in midair. The leaders were very decent fellows and pulled up as soon as I called.

"Squatting on my lump of seaweed like a turtle"

" 'Where will I get to anyway if I keep going straight along this current?' I asked.

" 'Oh, great heavens!' they said. 'That current meanders all the way down into the Antarctic. Where do you want to get to?'

" 'The nearest land—now, I suppose,' said I. 'I'm dead beat and can't go many more hours without something to eat and a real rest.'

" 'Well, turn and cut right across the current, then,' said

they, 'to your left as you're flying now. That'll bring you to Ebony Island. Keep high up and you can't miss it. It's got mountains. That's the nearest land. About a two-hour fly. So long!'

"Without wasting further daylight—for it was now getting late in the afternoon—I took the finches' advice and headed away to the left of the current in search of Ebony Island. This time I kept direction by flying square across the drifting chains of seaweed instead of following their course.

"Well, it may have been only a two-hour trip for those finches, but it was a very different thing for me. After three hours of steady going my wing began to trouble me again. The big setting sun was already standing on the skyline like an enormous plate. It would be dark in twenty minutes more. Here the seaweed was no longer visible. I had passed beyond the path of the current. And still no land had come in sight. I took a sort of bearing by the position of the sun and plugged along.

"Darkness came, but with it came a star. It twinkled out of the gloomy sky right ahead of me as the sun disappeared beneath the sea's edge. And although I knew that the stars do not stand still I reckoned that this one couldn't move very much in a couple of hours, and that was certainly as long as I would be able to keep going with a groggy wing. So, heading straight for that guiding silver point in a world of blackness, I plowed on.

"Another hour went by. Weary and winded, I now began to wonder if the finch leader could have made a mistake. He had said there were mountains on the island. As more and more stars had come twinkling out into the gloomy bowl of the sky, the night had grown lighter. And although there was no moon, the air was clear of mist and I could see the horizon all around me. Still no land!

"Maybe I'm not high enough, I thought. With a tremendous effort I tilted my head upward, and still plowing forward on the line of my big star, I raised my level a thousand feet or so. And suddenly, slightly to the left of my direction, I spied something white and woolly-looking, apparently floating between sky and sea.

"That surely can't be land! I thought. White in color! It looks more like clouds.

"Presently as I flapped along like a machine, just dumb and stupid with weariness, exhaustion, and thirst, strange new smells began to reach me—vaguely and dimly—sort of spicy odors, things that I hadn't smelled before, but which I knew did not belong to the sea. My floating clouds grew bigger as I approached. As I realized how high up in the sky they hung I became surer than ever that they were just white clouds or mist. Then the air seemed to change its temperature fitfully. Little drafts and breezes, now warm, now freezing cold, beat gently in my face.

"And then! At last I saw that my clouds were not floating at all. They were connected with the sea, but that which they stood on, being darker in color, had been invisible till I got close. The white snow-capped tops of mountains glistering in the dim starlight had beckoned to me across the sea. From the icy wastes of the upper levels had come the chilly winds; but down lower, now visible right under me, tangled sleeping jungles of dark green sent forth the fragrance of spices and tropical fruits. I was hovering over Ebony Island.

"With a cry of joy I shut my aching wings and dropped like a stone through the eight thousand feet of air, which grew warmer and warmer as I came down.

"I landed beside a little purling stream that carried the melting snows of the peaks down through the woodlands

"The white snow-capped tops of mountains had beckoned to me"

to the sea. And wading knee deep in the cold fresh water I bathed my tired wings and drank and drank and drank!

"In the morning, after a good sleep, I went forth to hunt for food and explore my new home. Nuts and seeds and fruit I found in abundance. The climate was delightful, hot down by the sea—quite hot—but you could get almost any temperature you fancied just by moving to the higher levels up the mountains. It was uninhabited by people and almost entirely free from birds of prey. What there were

were fish eagles—who would not bother me—and one or two kinds of owls, who preferred mice to small birds. I decided that it was an ideal place that I had come to.

" 'So!' I said, 'here I will settle down and live an old maid. No more will I bother my head about fickle mates. I'm a mongrel, anyway. Never again will I risk being deserted for a thoroughbred minx. I'll be like Aunt Rosie—live alone and watch the world pass by, and the year go around in peace. Poof! What do I care for all the cocks in the world! This beautiful island belongs to me. Here will I live and die, a crossbred but dignified hermit.'

"My island was large and its scenery varied. There were always new parts to explore—mountains, valleys, hillsides, meadows, jungle, sedgy swamps, golden-sanded, laughing shores, and little inland lakes. Later, as I came to the shore on the far side, I could see in the distance another piece of land. I decided it must be another island such as the one on which I had landed.

"Later I explored this island too and found it only one of many more that lay in sort of a chain. There was no end of variety in scenery and beautiful flowers, and I began to think of the whole string of islands as belonging to me. I composed some beautiful poetry and many excellent songs and kept my voice in good form practicing scales three hours a day.

"But all my verses had a melancholy ring. I couldn't seem to convince myself that living alone like this was the happiest way to exist. That was the first sign I had that something funny was happening to me.

" 'Look here,' I said. 'This won't do. Even if you're going to be an old maid you needn't be a sour old maid. This is a beautiful and cheerful island. Why be sad?'

"And I set deliberately to work to make up a cheerful

song. It went all right for the first two or three verses, but it ended mournfully, like the rest.

"Then I tried to get acquainted with the other finches and small birds that lived on the island. They were very hospitable and nice to me. And the cocks vied with one another to be seen in my company.

"And then the window cleaner kept coming to my mind."

"Ah!" said Gub-Gub. But Jip promptly put a large paw over his mouth and Pippinella went on.

"In some mysterious way, my good friend of the windmill . . . well, I can't quite explain it, but it almost seemed at times as though I felt him near me, somewhere. I spent hours and hours working out all the things that could have happened to him—that might have prevented him from coming back that night when he left me hanging on the wall exposed to the storms of heaven.

"And then it suddenly occurred to me that I should never have left the neighborhood of the mill. Something told me that he wasn't dead. And if he were still alive he would certainly return someday—the first moment that he could. And I should have been there to welcome him back—as I always had done when he returned from work. I started to blame myself.

" 'If you had been a dog,' I said, 'you would never have come away. You would have stayed on and on, knowing that you could trust him—knowing that if he still lived, in the end he would come back.' "

· The Fourth Chapter ·
PIPPINELLA FINDS A CLUE

HE NEXT evening as the Dolittle household took their places at the little table in the wagon to hear the continuation of the canary's story, Gub-Gub appeared to be in a great state of excitement. He was the first to sit down. He provided himself with an extra high cushion and he kept whispering to the neighbors.

"The window cleaner's coming back this time. I know it. Goodness! He has taken an age, hasn't he? But it's all right. He wasn't killed. He's coming back into the story tonight, sure as you're alive."

"Sh!" said the Doctor, tapping his notebook with a pencil.

When everyone was settled Pippinella hopped up onto the tobacco box and began.

"One day, about a week after I had left the company of the other birds and returned to my solitary life, I decided to fly over to the small island that lay south of Ebony Island. Perhaps it would help to take my mind off my loneliness, for my friend the window cleaner was still very much in my thoughts. It was the first clear day we had had in weeks, and I was able to see again the shore of the smaller island. I came to a place where big shoulders of rocks jutted down right into the sea. In such places as this, little berry bushes often grew. I flew up onto the rocks to hunt for fruit. On the top I found a flat, level place from which you could get a fine view of the sea in front. Behind, one of the mountains rose straight, like a wall. And in the face of this wall of rock there was an opening to a cave.

"Out of idle curiosity I went into the cave to explore it. It wasn't very deep. I hopped around the floor a while and then started to come out. Suddenly I stood stock-still, my attention held spellbound by a stick that leaned against the wall of the cave with a square piece of rag tied to its top, like a flag. It was the rag that held me there, gazing motionless with open bill and staring eyes. For I knew that rag as well as I knew my own feathers. It was the cloth my friend the window cleaner used to clean windows with!

"How often had I studied it as he rubbed it over the glass not more than six inches from my nose at Aunt Rosie's! How many times had I watched him wash it out in the kitchen sink at the windmill when he returned from work and then hang it up to dry, close to my cage over the stove! I remembered that it had a rent close to one corner, which had been stitched up clumsily with heavy thread. I sprang up onto the top of the stick and pulled its hanging folds out with my bill. And there was the mended tear. There could be no mistake. It was my window cleaner's rag.

"Suddenly I found myself weeping. Just why I didn't know. But one thing was made clear to me at last! I knew now why I couldn't settle down a happy old maid; I knew why all my songs were sad; I knew why I couldn't content myself with the company of the other island birds. I was lonely for people. It was natural. I had been born and bred a cage bird. I had grown to love the haunts of men. And all this time I had been longing to get back to them. I thought of all the good people—friends that I had known—old Jack, the merry driver of the night coach from the north; the kindly Marchioness who lived in the castle; the scarred-faced old sergeant and my comrades of the Fusiliers; and, finally, the one I had loved the best of all, the odd, studious window cleaner who wrote books in a windmill. What had I to do with the blue and yellow macaws that climbed the orchid vines in gorgeous jungle land? People was what I wanted. And he had been here; the one I wanted most had lived in this cave! Yet I was certain, after my thorough exploration of the island, that he was here no longer. Where—where was he now?

"After that I thought of nothing else but getting away—or getting back to civilization and the haunts of men. I would return, I was determined, to the windmill, and there I would wait till my friend the window cleaner made his way to his old home.

"I returned to the main island and prepared to set out for home. But the autumn equinox was just beginning. For days on end strong winds blew across my island and whipped the sea into a continuous state of unrest. Such birds as passed over were all going the wrong way for me. Once again I, the exile, the cage bird, was trying to make my way against the current, instead of with it.

"I was afraid, alone, and inexperienced, to pit my feeble strength against tempestuous weather. This time I was not desperate or in any such foolhardy state of mind as when I launched out after I left Nippit. Now life meant much; the future held promise. And if I were to get back to my window-cleaner philosopher I must not take any crazy chances.

"For days I watched the sea, waiting for calmer weather. But the blustering winds continued, and when I tried my strength against them over the land, to see if I could make any headway, I found that I was like a feather and they could drive me where they would.

"One afternoon when I was sitting on the rocks looking out to sea, I saw a big ship come over the horizon. The wind had changed its direction earlier in the day, and now, with a powerful breeze behind it, this boat was traveling along at quite a good speed. It seemed to be going pretty much the way I wanted. And it occurred to me that if I followed this boat I might easily come to the land I had left. At the worst, if I got exhausted, I would have something to land on.

"The ship came nearer and nearer. At one time I thought it was actually going to call at the islands. But I was wrong. When it had come within less than half a mile of a steep mountainous cape at one corner it changed its course slightly, rounded the angle of the coast, and passed on. At that close range I could see men moving on the deck. The sight of them made me more homesick than ever for human company. As the boat grew smaller, moving away from me now, I made up my mind. I leapt off the rocks and shot out over the sea to follow it.

"Well, I was still a pretty inexperienced navigator. I very soon found out that my little plan, which had sounded perfectly simple, just didn't work. For one thing, on the side of the island where I had been standing one was protected from the weather. And it was only after I had gotten well out away from the shore that the full strength of the wind hit me. When it had changed it had changed for the worse —growing stronger with its new direction. Across the sky rain clouds gathered. Rumbles of thunder warned me that I should never have attempted this mad excursion.

"Further, on getting close to the boat, I found that its pace was dreadfully slow, in spite of the wind behind it. It was pitching clumsily in the swell and seemed heavy laden. If it had taken me a whole day to make the voyage at seventy miles an hour it would take this vessel a week at least. During that week I would be starved to death twice over. I realized in a moment that my plan was no good. I must head back for the island and reach it before that drenching shower reached me.

"I turned. And, oh, my! I thought I had known how strong that wind was. But I hadn't any idea of it until I swung around and faced it. It was a veritable gale. I flapped my wings as fast as I could, and the only result I got was to stand still. Even that I couldn't keep up. And soon, slowly, I found I was moving backward while working like mad to get forward.

"And then, *slish!* The rain squall hit me in the face, and in a moment I was drenched to the skin.

"So there I was, fairly caught, a good three miles off shore, unable to regain the land in the teeth of that terrible wind. What a fool I had been to leave my snug, safe harbor before calm weather came!

"The soaking of the rain squall made flying doubly hard. After a few moments of it I decided not to try to beat into the wind at all. That was hopeless. I must wait till the fury of the gale let up. In the meantime I was compelled to give all my attention to keeping up above the level of the sea, for with my drenched and soggy feathers I found myself descending all the time nearer and nearer to the tossing surface of the water.

"But far from weakening, the force of the wind got suddenly stronger. I felt myself now being swept along like a leaf. The curtain of the rain had shut out all view of the island. You couldn't see more than a few yards in any direction. Above and below and around all was gray—just gray wetness.

"As the wind hurled me along over the sea I presently

caught sight of the ship. The gale was driving me right past it—beyond, into the hopeless waste of the angry ocean. I remember the picture of it very clearly as it hove up in the dim veil of rain. It looked like a great gray horse mired and floundering in a field of gray mud. I suddenly realized that this vessel was my last and only chance. If I got driven beyond it, it was all up with me.

"Frantically I flapped at the wet air to change the angle of my flight—to descend sideways and strike the vessel's deck.

"Well, somehow I managed it. As the squall drove me through the rigging I clutched at a rope ladder stretched between the rail and the masthead. I grabbed it with my claws and threw my wings around it, rather like a monkey climbing on a pole. For the present I didn't attempt to move up or down. I decided to let good enough alone. I was on the ship. That was the main thing. I would stay where I was until the rain shower passed on.

"By that time I was just numbed with the cold and the wet. The air cleared and the sun came out, as it does, suddenly, after those squalls at sea. But still the wind held very strong. I set about making my way down to some more sheltered place. For the first time I had a chance to look around me and take in the details of the ship I had boarded. I was about seven feet above the level of the deck. Not far away from me there was a sort of a little house with round windows and a door in it. If I could get close up against the wall of this, I thought, I would be protected from the wind and would still have the sunshine to dry my feathers in. I was afraid to fly the short distance, lest the wind catch me up and carry me overboard. So, like a sailor, I started climbing down my rope ladder hand over hand.

"In my hurry to get to some warmer, safer place I had

not noticed much about the ship beyond just a glimpse that told me it was a vessel of considerable size. And on my way down the rope I was much too busy clinging tight and battling with the wind—which seemed determined to tear me loose and hurl me into the sea—to notice anything around me.

"Anyway, suddenly I felt a large hand close around my whole body and lift me off the rope like a fly. I looked up and found myself staring into the brown face of an enormous sailor dressed in a tarpaulin coat and hat. A wild bird, I suppose, would have been scared to death. But I had often been held in people's hands before and that in itself did not greatly alarm me. The sailor had kind eyes and I knew he would do me no harm. But I also knew that this probably meant the end of my freedom for the present because sailors are fond of pets and most ships have one cage at least of canaries aboard them.

" 'Hulloa, hulloa!' said the big man. 'What'cher climbing in the rigging for? Don't you know no better than that? You ain't been to sea long, I'll warrant. Why, if we was to ship water with you tightrope-walking like that you'd go overboard before you could blink! I reckon you signed on as we passed the island, eh? Well, well! Bless me, ain't you wet! You come below, mate, and get dried out where it's snug and warm!'

"Then the man moved forward across the pitching, rolling deck to the little house and opened the door. Inside there was a flight of steps and down this he carried me. We entered a small, low room, with beds set in the wall all around, like shelves. A lamp hung from the center of the ceiling and swung from side to side with the motion of the ship. On the tables and chairs coats and capes had been thrown. There was a warm smell of tar and tobacco and

" 'Bless me, ain't you wet!' "

wet clothes. In two of the bunks men were snoring, with their mouths open.

"My captor, still holding me firmly in his hand, opened a heavy wooden locker and brought forth a small cage. Into this he put me and then filled the drawer with seed and the pot with water.

" 'There you are, mate,' says he. 'Now you're all fixed up. Get your feathers dry and then you'll feel better.'

"And so I entered on still another chapter in my varied

career. After the dead quiet of the island, the cheerful bustle of that ship was most invigorating. It was, as I have told you, quite a large vessel, and it carried both cargo and passengers. To begin with, my cage was kept in that little cabin to which I had first been taken. It was a kind of bunkroom for the crew. There was nearly always somebody sleeping there, because the men took it in turn in batches to work the ship.

"Later, when the weather got fair, I was put outside on the wall of the little deckhouse. This was much nicer. Lots and lots of people came to talk to me—especially the passengers, who seemed to have nothing to do to occupy their time beyond walking up and down the deck in smart clothes.

"And although I was terribly annoyed at being caged up again, I counted myself lucky that I had escaped the dangers of the sea when escape seemed impossible. There was always a good chance that I might still get away and reach the windmill—after we got to land—if I kept my eye open for the opportunity. In the meantime, I was back again among pleasant people and agreeable scenes.

"There was another canary aboard the ship. I heard him singing the first day that I was put outside on the deck. Singing is hardly the word for it, for he poor fellow had only a few squeaky calls without any melody to them. But he was very persevering and seemed determined to work up a song of some kind. Just whereabouts on the vessel he was I couldn't make out—nearer amidships than I was, by the sound of it. His unmusical efforts sort of annoyed me after a while and presently I gave a performance myself—more to drown his racket in self-defense than anything else.

"But my singing caused something of a sensation.

Passengers—and even sailors, stewards, and officers—
gathered around to listen to me. Inquiries were made as to
whom I belonged. And finally I was bought from the big
sailor who had caught me and taken to quite a different
part of the ship.

"The man who bought me turned out to be the ship's
barber. I was carried to a little cabin on the main deck,
right in the center of the passengers' quarters. This was the
barbershop, all fitted up with shaving chairs and basins,
like a regular hairdressing establishment on land.

"And there I discovered the other canary, hanging in a
cage from the ceiling. It was the barber's idea, apparently,
that I should teach this other bird how to sing.

"I was now in a very much better position to keep in
touch with the life of the ship than I was before. For nearly
everyone on board came, sooner or later, to the barbershop. My new master was patronized not only by the passengers, but the officers and even the crew, in the early
hours of the morning before the shop was supposed to be
open, came to be shaved or to have their hair cut.

"And while the customers were being attended to or
waiting their turn, the barber would chat and gossip with
them. And from their conversation I learned a good deal.
And then the other canary, the funny little squeaker to
whom I was supposed to give singing lessons, he had been
on the ship quite a number of voyages, and he, too, gave
me a lot of information.

"He was a really decent sort of a bird—even if he
couldn't sing. And he explained many things to me about
the life of the sea and the running of a ship that I had
never known before. As for teaching him to sing, that was
a pretty hopeless task, for he had no voice to speak of at
all. Still, he improved a good deal, and after about a week

his gratey squeaks and shrill whistles were not nearly so harsh to the ear.

"One song that I composed at this time I was rather proud of. I called it 'The Razor Strop Duet.' Listening to the barber stropping his razor gave me the idea, the motif, for it. You know the *clip-clop, clip-clop, clip-clop* that a razor makes when it is sharpened on leather? Well, I imitated that and mixed it up with the sound of a shaving brush lathering in a mug. But it was a little difficult to do the two with one voice. So I did the razor, and I made the other canary do the shaving brush. As a song it could not compare with some of my other compositions—with 'The Midget Mascot,' for instance, or 'The Harness Jingle.' It was a sort of comic song, 'The Razor Strop Duet.' But it was a great success and the barber was forever showing us off to his customers by giving his razor an extra stropping, for he knew that that would always set us going.

"I questioned the other canary very minutely as to the places we would touch and about our port of destination. For all this time, you must understand, I had one idea very much in mind—to escape from my cage and the ship as soon as we dropped anchor in a convenient harbor. I gathered from what he told me that our next port of call was the land that I had left—the land of the windmill and the window cleaner.

"Continually now I was trying my utmost to show the barber how tame I was. When he cleaned out the cage I would hop onto his finger. And after a little he would sometimes close the doors and windows and allow me to go free in the room. I would fly from the floor to the table onto his hand. And finally he would let me out even with the doors open. This was what I wanted. I did not attempt to escape yet, of course, because we were still at sea. And whenever he wished me to return into the cage I would go back as good as gold.

"But I was only biding my time. When we were in port he would, if all went well, let me out of my cage once too often."

· The Fifth Chapter ·

THE WINDOW CLEANER AT LAST!

ONE DAY toward evening there was a great commotion on the deck. Passengers were running forward with spyglasses and pointing over the sea. Land had been sighted. We were now only half an hour or so from the port where I hoped to escape.

"As we neared the land men came out in boats to guide us into the harbor. There was no end of signaling and shouting between the ship and the shore and finally, when we did creep in at a snail's pace, they tied the vessel down from every angle. I could not help comparing all this with the carefree, simple manner in which birds make their landing in a new country, after a voyage of many thousands of miles.

"From my position hanging inside the barbershop I could not see a great deal of the port in which we had come, beyond little glimpses through the door and porthole. But from them I recognized the place. It was a town not more than fifty miles from the hill on which the windmill stood. Shortly after we were moved up to a wharf some friends of the barber came aboard to see him. They sat around drinking beer and chatting and presently one of them said to him, 'I see you've got another canary, Bill.'

" 'Yes,' said the barber. 'A good singer, too. And he's that tame he'll come right out onto my hand. Wait a minute and I'll show you.'

"Aha! I thought to myself. Now my chance is coming.

"Then the barber opened my cage door and, standing a few paces off, he held out his hand and called to me to fly out onto it. Through the open door of the shop I could see part of the town, steep streets straggling up toward hills and pleasant rolling pastureland. I hopped onto the sill of my cage and stood a moment, half in and half out.

" 'Now, watch him,' called the barber to his friends. 'He'll fly right onto my finger. He's done it lots of times. Come on, Dick! Here I am. Come on!'

"And then I flew—but not onto his finger. Taking a line on those steep streets that I could see in the distance straggling up the hill, I made for the open door.

"But, alas! Such off chances can upset the best plans! Just as I was about to skim through the doorway it was suddenly blocked by an enormous figure. It was my big sailor. Of course, it would be—pretty nearly the largest man that ever walked, coming through the smallest doorway ever built. There were just two narrow little places either side of his head through which I might get by him. I tilted upward and made for one of them.

" 'Look out!' yelled the barber. 'The bird's getting away. Grab him!'

"But the big sailor had already seen me. As I tried to slip out over his shoulder he clapped his two big hands together and caught me just like a ball that had been thrown to him.

"And that was the end of my great hopes and careful

HUGH LOFTING

"I stood half in, half out"

scheming! Because, of course, after that the barber never trusted me out with the door or windows open again. I was put back into the cage, and there I stayed.

"Well, after six or seven hours the ship began to make ready to put to sea again.

" 'What's the next port of call at which we stop?' I asked the other canary.

" 'Oh, a long ways on,' said he. 'We go pretty nearly the whole length of the sea we're in now and touch at a group of islands at the mouth of a narrow strait. It takes nine days. But the islands are very pretty and worth seeing.'

"But what did I care for the beauty of the islands! As the ropes were untied and the vessel moved out away from the wharf I saw the steep streets growing smaller. Beside myself with disappointment and annoyance, I beat the bars of my cage in senseless fury. I was sailing away from my friend, from the land of the windmill. And now, with my owner suspicious, heaven only knew when I'd ever have a chance to get back to it again!

"For the next three days our voyage was uneventful. Calm sunny weather prevailed, and the barbershop was kept quite busy.

"On the fourth day we had a little excitement. A wreck was sighted. Unfortunately my cage was not hung outside that day, and I could see practically nothing of the show. But from conversation and a little guesswork on my part I managed to piece most of the story together.

"About noon some kind of craft was seen by the man in the crow's nest—as the lookout on the mast is called. It was evidently in distress. There was a lot of signaling and a good deal of running about and looking through telescopes. Our ship's course was changed and we headed in the direction of the stranger.

"On closer inspection it was found not to be a wreck but a raft with one man on it. The man was either unconscious or dead. He lay face downward and gave no answer when he was hailed. A boat was lowered and he was brought aboard. There was much cheering among the passengers when it was announced that he was still breathing. He was, nevertheless, in a terrible state of exhaustion from hunger and exposure. He was handed over into the care of the ship's doctor, and, still unconscious, was taken below and put to bed. Then our boat was set back upon her course and on we went.

"I thought no more about the incident after the customers who came to the barber's had ceased to talk about it.

"One day about a week later, when we were supposed to be getting near our next port of call, a most extraordinary-looking man entered the barbershop. His strange appearance seemed to cause him a good deal of embarrassment. Without looking around at all, he sat down in the barber's chair. The barber must have expected him. For he set to work at once, without asking any questions, shaving off his beard and cutting his hair. The man's back was turned to me as he sat in the chair, and all I could see of him after the white apron was tied about his chin, was the top of his wild-looking head of tangled, matted hair.

"In the middle of the clipping and shaving the barber went to the door to speak to someone. And I gathered from the conversation that the man in the chair was the poor wolf who had been saved from the raft. He was only now recovered enough to leave his bed for the first time. This made me more interested in him than ever. And, entirely fascinated, I watched in silence as the barber clipped away at that enormous shock of hair. I fell to wondering what he would look like when that beard had been removed.

"At last the barber finished and with a flick and a flourish removed the apron from around his customer's neck. Weakly the man got out of the chair and stood up. He turned around and I saw his face.

"You could never guess who it was."

"The window cleaner!" yelled Gub-Gub, slipping off his cushion and disappearing under the table in his excitement.

"Yes," said Pippinella quietly, "it was the window cleaner."

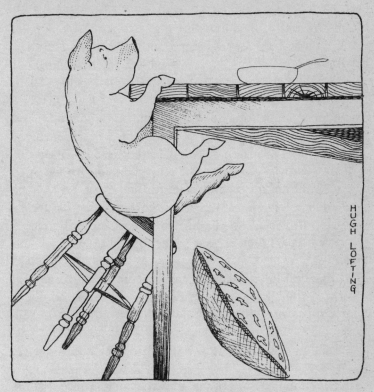

" 'The window cleaner!' yelled Gub-Gub"

Gub-Gub's sudden disappearance caused a short interruption, and some two or three minutes were spent fishing him out from under the table and putting him and his cushion back on the stool. There, slightly bruised but otherwise none the worse for his accident, he continued to show intense interest in the canary's story while occasionally rubbing the side of his head, which he had bumped on the leg of the table.

"Well," Pippinella continued, "I was greatly shocked at

my friend's appearance. I recognized him, beyond all doubt, instantly, of course. But, oh, so thin he looked, pale, weary, and weak! As yet he had not noticed me. Standing by the barber's chair, embarrassed, staring awkwardly at the floor, he started to put his hand in his pocket. Then, seeming to remember halfway that he had no money, he murmured something to the barber in explanation and hurried to leave the shop.

"There was a certain call that I used to give—a kind of greeting whistle—whenever he returned in days gone by to the windmill of an evening after his work was over. As he took hold of the door handle to go out onto the deck I repeated it twice. Then he turned around and saw me.

"Never have I seen anyone's face so light up with joy and gladness.

" 'Oh, Pip!' he cried, coming close up to my cage and peering in. 'Is it really you? Yes. There could be no doubt about those markings. I could pick you out from a million!'

" 'Pardon me,' said the barber. 'Do you know my canary?'

" '*Your* canary!' said the window cleaner. 'There is some mistake here. This bird is mine. I am quite sure of it.'

"And then began a long argument. Of course, quite naturally, the barber wasn't going to give me up just on the other man's say-so. The sailor who had first caught me was called in. Then various stewards and other members of the crew joined the discussion. My friend, the window cleaner, was very polite through it all, but very firm. He was asked how long ago it was that I had been in his possession. And when he said it was many months since he had seen me last the others all laughed at him, saying that his claim was simply ridiculous. Never have I wished harder that I could talk the language of people, so that I might explain to them beyond all doubt which one was my real owner.

"Well, finally the matter was taken to the captain. Already many of the passengers were interested in the argument and when he came down to the barbershop the place was crowded with people who were all giving advice and taking sides.

"The captain began by telling everybody to keep quiet while he heard both versions of the story. Then the barber and the window cleaner in turn put forward their claims, giving reasons and particulars and all the rest. Next, the big sailor stated how he had found me in the rigging during a rain squall and had taken me below and later sold me to the barber.

"When they had all done the captain turned to the window cleaner and said, 'I don't see how you can claim ownership of the bird on such evidence. There could easily be many birds marked the same as this one. The chances are that this was a wild bird that took refuge on this ship during bad weather. In the circumstances I feel that the barber has every right to keep it.'

"Well, that seemed to be the end of the matter. The question had been referred to the captain, the highest authority on the ship, and he had decided in favor of the barber. It looked as though I were going to remain in his possession.

"But the window cleaner and his romantic rescue from the sea had greatly interested the passengers. His face was the kind of face that everyone would instinctively trust as honest. Many people felt that he would not have laid claim to me with such sureness and determination if he were not really my owner. And as the captain stepped out onto the deck one of the passengers—a funny, fussy old gentleman with side-whiskers—followed him and touched him on the arm.

" 'Pardon me, captain,' said he. 'I have a feeling that our castaway is an upright and honorable person. If his claim to the canary should be just, possibly the bird will know him. Perhaps he can even do tricks with it. Would it not be as well to try some test of that kind before dismissing the case?'

"The captain turned back and all the other passengers who had been leaving now reentered the barbershop, their interest reviving at the prospect of a new trial.

" 'Listen,' said the captain, addressing the window cleaner: 'You say you know the canary well. Does the bird know you at all? Is there anything you can do to prove that what you say is true?'

" 'Yes, the bird knows me, sir,' said the barber. 'He'll hop right out of the cage onto my hand when I call him. If you'll shut the door I'll show you.'

" 'Very good,' said the captain. 'Close the door.'

"Then, with the little cabin crowded with people, the barber opened my cage, held up his hand, and called to me to come out. I did—and, of course, flew straight to the window cleaner's shoulder.

"A whisper of astonishment ran around among the passengers. Then I climbed off my friend's shoulder and clawed my way down his waistcoat. I wanted to remind him of an old trick he used to do with me at the mill. At supper he would sometimes put a lump of sugar in his waistcoat pocket and I would fish it out and drop it in his teacup. As soon as I started to walk down off his shoulder he remembered it and asked for a lump of sugar and a cup. They were brought forward by a steward. Then he explained to the captain what he was going to do, put the sugar in his pocket and the teacup on the barber's washstand.

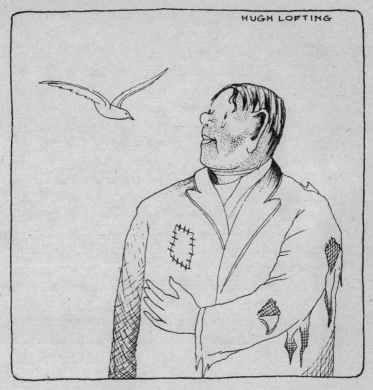

"I flew straight to the window cleaner's shoulder"

"Well, I wish you could have seen the barber's face when I pulled that sugar out, flew to the cup, and dropped it in.

" 'Why, captain,' cried the old gentleman with the side-whiskers, 'there can be no question now, surely, as to who is the owner. The bird will do anything for this man. I thought he wouldn't have claimed it if it weren't his own.'

" 'Yes,' said the captain, 'the canary is his. There can be no doubt of that.'

"And amid much talking and congratulations from the

passengers the window cleaner prepared to take me away. Then came the question of the ownership of the cage. That belonged to the barber, of course. But as there was no other empty one to be had aboard the ship my friend couldn't very well take me without it. However the old gentleman with the side-whiskers, who seemed genuinely interested in the strange story of my funny owner and my-self, came forward and volunteered to pay the barber the value of the cage.

"The window cleaner thanked him and asked him for his name and address. He hadn't any money now, he said, but he wanted to send it to him after he got to land. Then I and my friend from whom I had been separated so long left the barbershop and proceeded to the forward part of the ship, where he had his quarters.

" 'Well, Pip,' said he, shaking up the mattress of his bed, 'here we are again! The captain's been pretty generous. Gave me a first-class cabin for nothing. Of course, I can't expect to have the services of a steward as well. So I make my own bed—where the dickens did that pillow get to? Oh, there it is, on the floor . . . Poor old Pip! What ages it is since we talked to each other. And then to find you aboard the ship that rescued me, living in the barbershop! Dear, dear, what a strange world it is, to be sure! There goes five bells. That means half past six. It'll soon be dinnertime. Are you hungry, Pip? Let's see. Oh, no, you've got plenty of seed. And I'll bring you a piece of apple from the dining saloon. What a decent chap that bewhiskered old fellow was, wasn't he—paying for your cage and all like that? Heaven only knows when he'll get his money back. I haven't a penny in the world. But I must see that he gets it somehow.'

"While he finished making the bed he went on vaguely

about this and that, gradually coming to the part I wanted to hear the most.

" 'Pip,' he said finally in a more confidential tone. 'I sometimes believe you understand every word I say. Do you know why? Whenever I talk, you keep silent. Is it possible you *do* know what I am saying?'

"I tried to make a sound similar to the human word for yes but it just came out a peep, which surprised him a little for he looked at me sharply and smiled.

" 'Never mind, Pip,' he said. 'Whether you understand or not I still get great comfort from talking to you. Oh, goodness, I feel weak!' he said, dropping down onto the bunk. 'I better sit down a while. The least exertion tires me out now. I haven't gotten over that starving and the sun. Listen, Pip, would you like to know the real reason why I never came back to the mill that night? Just a minute . . .'

"He went over to the door, opened it, and looked out.

" 'It's all right,' he said, coming back to his seat on the bunk. 'There's no one eavesdropping.'

"His voice sank to a whisper as he leaned forward toward my cage, which stood on a table near his bunk. He seemed to be suddenly overcome with a spell of dizziness, for he closed his eyes a moment. I felt that he really ought to be in bed, recovering from his trip. But I felt proud because I realized that what he was about to tell me had most likely never been told to a living soul."

· The Sixth Chapter ·
THE WINDOW CLEANER'S ADVENTURES

OU remember those books I used to write, Pip?' the window cleaner began. 'Well, they were books about governments—foreign governments. Before you knew me—before I was a window cleaner—I had traveled the world a great deal. And in many countries I found that the people were not treated well. I tried to speak about it. But I wasn't allowed to. So I decided that I would go back to my own land and write about it. And that is what I did. I wrote in newspapers and magazines. But the government there didn't like the sort of thing I wrote—although it had not been written against them exactly. They sent to the editors of these magazines and newspapers and asked them not to allow me to write for them anymore.'

" 'In those days I had a great many friends—and a good deal of money, too, for I was born of quite wealthy parents. But when my friends found that I was getting into hot water with the government, many of them wouldn't be seen with me anymore. Some of them thought I was just a harmless crank, sort of crazy, you know—the way people always do regard you if you do anything different from the herd.'

" 'And so,' he went on, 'I set out to disappear. One day I took a boat and went for a row on the sea. When there was no one around I upset the boat and swam to shore. Then I made my way secretly on foot a long distance from those parts and was never seen again by any of my friends or relatives. Of course, when the upturned boat was found people decided that I had been drowned. Most of my money and houses and property went to my younger brother as the next of kin, and very soon I was forgotten.'

" 'In the meantime I had become a window cleaner in the town where you met me. I rented that old ramshackle mill from a farmer for two shillings a month. And there I settled down to write the books with which I hoped to change the world. I have never been so happy in my life as I was there, Pip. I had never been so free before. And the first book that I wrote did change things—even more than I expected. It was printed in a foreign country and read by a great number of people. They decided that what I wrote was true. And they began to make a whole lot of fuss and to try to change their government.'

" 'But they were not quite strong enough and their attempt failed. In the meantime the government of that particular country got very busy trying to find out who had written the book that caused so much trouble and nearly lost them their jobs.'

"At that point," Pippinella continued, "the window cleaner was interrupted by the ringing of six bells and the bugle for dinner. He excused himself and left the cabin.

"In about half an hour he returned, bringing with him a piece of apple, a stump of celery, and some other tidbits from the table for me. While he was putting them in my cage the ship's doctor came to see him. He was still, of course, more or less under his care. The doctor examined my friend and seemed satisfied with his progress. But on leaving he ordered him to go to bed early and to avoid all serious exertion for the present.

"After the doctor had gone my friend started to undress, and I supposed that I should have no more of the story for the present. But after he had got into bed he continued talking to me. I have since thought that this was perhaps a sign that he was still very weak from all he had gone through. It seemed as though he just had to talk—but he was afraid to do it when there were any people around to hear him. So, I, the canary, was his audience.

" 'How that foreign government,' he went on, 'found out that it was I who wrote the books I do not know to this day. But I suppose they must have traced my letters because, after calling at the post office that Saturday when I left you outside on the wall, I was followed by three men as I came away. I did not see them until it was too late. At a lonely part of the road leading back toward the mill I was struck to the ground with a blow on the head.

" 'When I woke up I was aboard a ship far out at sea. I demanded to know why I had been kidnapped. I was told that the ship was short of crew and they had to get an extra man somehow. This, of course, is—or was—often done by ships that were shorthanded. But from the start I was suspicious. The town they had taken me from was a long way from the sea. And no ship would send so far inland to shanghai sailors. Besides, nobody would ever take me for a seaman. Further I soon noticed that there was a group of foreigners on board; and later I learned that the port we were bound for was in that country about which I had written my book.

" 'I knew what would happen to me if I ever landed there; I would be arrested and thrown into prison on some false charge. So far as my relatives and friends were concerned, was I not dead long ago? No one in my own land would make inquiries. Once in the clutches of the government I had made an enemy of, I would never be heard of again.'

"The window cleaner lay back on his pillow as though exhausted from the effort of talking. He remained motionless so long that I began to think he had fallen asleep. And I was glad, because I did not want him to overtire himself. But presently he sat up again and drew my cage nearer to him across the table. With his feverish eyes burning more brightly than ever, he went on.

" 'As the ship carried me away one thing, Pip, besides my own plight worried me dreadfully. And that was you—you, my companion, my only friend. I had left your cage outside hanging on the wall. Would you be frozen to death by the cold night? Who would feed you? I remembered what a lonely place that old mill was. What chance was there that any passerby would see you? And even if he did, there would be nothing to show him, unless he broke in and found the kitchen empty, that you had been deserted. I imagined what you must be thinking of me as the hours and days went by—starving days and freezing nights— waiting, waiting for me to return, while all the time that accursed ship carried me farther and farther away! Poor Pip! Even now I can't believe it's you. Still, there you are, sure enough, with the yellow bars on your wings and the funny black patch across your throat and that cheeky trick of cocking your head on one side when you're listening— and—and everything.'

"And then, still murmuring fitfully, at last the window cleaner fell asleep. From my cage I looked at his haggard, pinched face on the pillow. I felt stupidly useless. I wished I were a person so I could take care of him and nurse him back to full health. For I realized now that he was still

"At last the window cleaner fell asleep"

dreadfully ill. However, it was a great deal to be with him again. I put my head under my wing and prepared to settle down myself. But I didn't get much rest. For all night long he kept jumping and murmuring in his sleep."

"But how did the window cleaner come to be on the raft?" whined Gub-Gub. "You've let him go to sleep now without telling us."

"Well, he hasn't gone to sleep forever," said the white mouse. "Give him a chance, can't you?"

"Oh, that pig," sighed Dab-Dab. "I don't know why we always have him in the party."

"Myself," growled Jip, "I'd sooner have a nice, smooth, round stone for company."

"Quiet, please!" said the Doctor. "Let Pippinella go on."

"Well," said the canary, "in the morning while he was dressing the window cleaner told me the rest of his story. Realizing that if he had remained on that ship till the end of its journey he would be cast into prison—probably for the rest of his days—he determined to escape from it at any cost before it reached port. He had been given work to do about the ship like the other sailors, so fortunately he was still free—in appearance, at all events. He bided his time and pretended not to be suspicious concerning his captors' intentions.

"After some days of sailing they passed an island at nighttime. The land was some three miles away at least, but its high mountain tops were visible in the moonlight. On account of the distance the men never dreamed that he would attempt to swim ashore. It was very late and no one was on deck. Taking a life belt from the rail my friend slipped quietly into the sea near the stern of the boat and struck out for the island.

"It was a tremendously long swim. And if it had not been for the belt, he told me, he could never have done it. But finally, more dead than alive from exhaustion, he staggered up onto the beach in the moonlight and lay down to rest and sleep."

Pippinella paused a moment while the whole Dolittle family waited eagerly for the rest of her story.

"I know!" shouted Gub-Gub. "Don't tell me. Let me guess. He landed on Ebony Island—the same as you did!"

"No," said the canary, shaking her head. "It would have been simple had he done that. No, the island on which he landed was one of the same group—but it lay two or three miles to the south of my island. I only found that out later as he described his further adventures."

"Incredible!" exclaimed John Dolittle. "Why, he must have been there at the same time you were living on the larger one. I know that group of islands well; they're close enough together to make visibility very good. Strange you didn't see him."

"Well, no, Doctor," replied the canary. "You see, it was the time of the fall rains and the sky was overcast and gray from one day to the next. I could never have seen him from my island. But you will remember that I told you I occasionally visited the other islands just to relieve the monotony. I must have been on his while he was on mine. You'll see, as my story progresses, how that could have happened."

"Quite so," said the Doctor. "Do go on Pippinella. I've never heard a more astonishing example of sheer coincidence."

"When the window cleaner awoke," continued the canary, "it was daylight and the first thing he saw was the ship about six or seven miles off, coming back to look for him.

"Fortunately he had lain down in the shadow of a big berry bush and had not yet been seen through the telescopes from the ship. Like a rabbit he made his way inland, keeping always in the cover of the underbrush. Reaching the far side of the island, he crept up into the higher mountain levels, where from vantage points he could see without being seen.

"He watched the vessel draw near and send boats ashore with search parties. Then began a long game of hide-and-seek. About two dozen men in all were brought onto the island. And from these twenty-four he had to remain hidden.

"All day long my friend watched like a hunted fox, peering out from the bushes and rocks at his pursuers. Darkness began to fall and he supposed that the men would now return to their ship. But to his horror he saw that they were settling down for the night, putting up bivouacs of boughs and lighting camp fires.

"For two days this continued. You might wonder why I didn't see the ship and the fires and the boats going back and forth from the ship to the shore. But it all must have taken place on the other side of the island—out of sight of where I stayed most of the time. And then, too, the fog was so thick that seeing more than a few feet in any direction was impossible.

"Finally, when it began to look as though his pursuers were never going to leave the island, my friend hit upon a plan. At nighttime he went down to the beach on that side of the island where the ship had come to anchor. You remember the life belt that he used to come ashore with?"

"Yes," said Gub-Gub, sneezing heartily.

"Well, he took that life belt, which had the ship's name written on it, and he flung it out beyond the surf. He watched it for a little to make sure that it was not washed back inshore, and then he made his way up again to his mountain retreats.

"Now at least once a day, sometimes more, boats passed between the island and the ship to get news of how the hunt was progressing or to bring supplies to the search parties. The following morning one of these boats sighted the life belt floating in the sea. It was captured and taken aboard the ship. When news of its discovery was brought

"He flung it out beyond the surf"

to the captain he decided that my friend had been drowned in his attempt to reach the island, and he signaled to the search parties to rejoin the ship.

"About half an hour later the window cleaner, watching from his mountain hiding places, saw the vessel weigh anchor and sail away. He described to me his great joy when he first realized that his plan had worked, that his enemies had at last departed and left him in peace. The first thing he did was to take a good sleep. Anxiety about the movements of his hunters had prevented his getting any real rest since he had seen the ship return.

"But after a while he found that his situation was by no means good, anyway. Immediate danger from the men who had kidnapped him was over, to be sure. But he was now marooned on an uninhabited island, with every prospect of staying there indefinitely. As week after week went by and he never even sighted the sail of a passing ship, he came to the conclusion that this island was far out of the paths of ocean traffic.

"All this time anxiety about the safety of his book added to his other troubles. He begrudged every day—every hour —spent here in useless idleness when his enemies might be busy behind his back, ransacking his home for the work on which he had labored so long.

"For food he subsisted on nuts, fish, and fruit, mostly. He took his quarters in that cave that I had explored. On the peak just above this he erected a flag made out of the cleaning rag that I found tied to the stick. This, he hoped, might catch the attention of some passing vessel. But none ever came.

"At last, when he had given up all hope of rescue from chance visitors, he decided that his only way of escape was to set out on a raft and try to get into the path of ships. So, somehow, with great patience, he fastened together a number of dry logs upon the beach. He fashioned a mast out of a pole and wove a sail by plating vines and leaves. Big seashells and other queer vessels were prepared to carry a supply of fresh water. He laid in a large store of nuts and bananas. When everything was ready, he thrust his raft out into the surf and prepared to sail away.

"But everything was against him. The weather, which had been fairly decent for some days, suddenly worsened just as he put out to sea. A violent wind blew the small, ill-fitted raft in a wide circle and flung it—all battered and broken—onto the beach of Ebony Island. Of course, he didn't realize at first that he wasn't back on his own island; he found it out only after he had dragged himself to shelter and waited out the storm.

"He told me how he began all over again to rebuild the raft; how he waited each day for some vessel to show up; and how, finally in desperation, he set out anyway.

"I don't know when I have ever heard," said Pippinella, "anything more terrible than the window cleaner's description of his voyage on that raft. With all his careful and thoughtful preparations, and because of the overcast sky, I suppose, he had neglected one important thing: some protection from the fierce rays of the sun. The first two days he had not realized his oversight, for a continual drift of light clouds across the sky shaded him even better than a parasol. But when on the third day the full glare of the tropical sun beat down on him, his little sailboat had made such good progress before the wind, that he calculated he was three hundred miles from the island and going back was out of the question.

"For five days the window cleaner drifted. By that time his fresh water was all gone and most of his food. A good deal of the time now he was out of his head entirely. He kept seeing imaginary ships appear on the skyline, he told me. He would get up and wave to them frantically, like a madman, then fall down in a state of utter collapse.

"Luckily he had not taken down his basketwork sail to use as a sunshade—sorely though he needed it. He was always hoping that a wind would come along and he feared that if he unlashed it from the mast he would not have strength to get it up again. It was this that saved him. Long after he had fallen unconscious for the last time it was sighted by the ship on which I was traveling. The

"He kept seeing imaginary ships"

captain told him afterward that it was very doubtful if the raft would have been seen at all if it had not been for that queer sail—which stood up high above the water.

" 'However,' the window cleaner said to me, 'all is well that ends well, Pip. Somehow my coming through this, my escape from the kidnappers, my rescue from the sea, make me feel I'm going to win through after all—so that the work I have begun will go forward to a successful end. It was a terrible experience. But I'm getting over it. And it has given me faith, Pip, faith in my star. I will yet upset that thieving government. I will yet live to see those people freed and happy.'

"That morning it was announced that we would most likely reach our next port the day after tomorrow. The kind old passenger with the side-whiskers still stuck to my friend, the window cleaner. He had gathered at the time of the discussion about the cage that my friend had no money. He came to our cabin later in the day and asked him what he proposed to do when he landed. The window cleaner shrugged his shoulders and, with a smile, said, 'Thank you, I don't just know exactly. But I'll manage somehow—get a job, I suppose, till I've made enough to buy a passage home.'

" 'But look here,' said the old gentleman, 'this port we're coming to is quite a small community, indeed. You'll have great difficulty, I fear, in securing employment. Besides, you're still far from well.'

"Nevertheless, my friend insisted, while thanking the other for his kind interest, that he would be able to get along somehow. But the old gentleman shook his head. And as he left the cabin he murmured, 'You're not strong enough yet. I must see if something can't be arranged.'

"That old gentleman reminded me a good deal of Aunt Rosie. He was one of those unfortunate elderly persons who, while apparently leading rather stupid lives, yet spend much time and thought doing good to others. He did arrange something, and that was a concert among the passengers. And the money they collected was presented to us. The window cleaner for a long time refused to take it. But in the end they made him.

"After thanking everybody aboard for his kindness, he was given a great send-off as he walked down the gangplank, his only baggage a birdcage beneath his arm. Both he and I were, I think, a little sorry to see the good ship weigh anchor and sail away. Certainly if it had not been for her hospitality both of us would have succumbed to the perils of the sea.

· The Seventh Chapter ·
THE RAGGED TRAMP

AFTER that we settled down to wait for a vessel homeward bound. We were told that a ship was expected in two weeks, but that it might be three before it came.

"This was a great disappointment to my friend, who was still itching to get back and find out the fate of his book. And it seemed as though the nearer he got to his goal the harder it became for him to wait.

" 'You see, the trouble is, Pip,' he kept on saying as he walked the sea wall with my cage beneath his arm, scanning the horizon for an approaching sail, 'the trouble is that mill is so unprotected. Those fellows could take up their quarters there and stay as long as they liked and no one would know the difference. And you can be sure, once they're certain they have found the house where I lived and wrote, they won't rest till they've discovered my papers.'

"Well, at last a ship came—a cargo vessel, pure and simple. My friend made arrangements with the captain to take us as far as a certain port in his own country. Some hours were spent in unloading freight and taking on supplies.

Finally, near nightfall, we got away. The window cleaner now appeared to throw care aside and regain something of his old habitual jolliness. It was the feeling of motion, action at last, after all the waiting that buoyed him up. As the vessel plowed merrily forward through the water he paced up and down the deck with a firmer, more vigorous manner than I had seen in him since we had rejoined one another.

"We had at least a two weeks' voyage ahead of us. My friend procured pens and ink and reams of paper. And hour after hour he would sit in his cabin, writing, writing, writing. He was describing his adventures with the agents or spies of the enemy government, he told me. He was going to add it to his book—if it still existed. Watching him scribbling away at his desk, stopping every once in a while to try to remember some detail of his life on the islands, or whatnot, gave me the idea to record in some way the story of my own life. For it was then, for the first time, that it occurred to me that perhaps my days had been adventurous enough to be worth telling.

"Now, I'm happy that I did. For if I had not composed those verses and songs it would not be so easy for me to recall all the details so that you could put them down in a regular book."

"Indeed," said the Doctor. "I'm glad you did too. This, I'm sure, will be a unique book—a real animal biography —such as I've wanted to do for so long. Shall we go on, or are you too tired?"

"Not at all," replied Pippinella. "I want to finish tonight, if possible.

"While the window cleaner scribbled away at his desk over the story of his kidnapping and escape at sea, I warbled away in my cage, trying out phrases and melodies till I had put together the whole song of my life in a manner that seemed musically fitting. Occasionally he would look up from his work and smile. He liked it. He always liked to hear me sing. But he seemed particularly struck by the love song of the greenfinch in the spring. It's funny how everyone seems to like that best. You remember yourself, John Dolittle, how when I sang for you that first time through the wrapping paper of my cage, it was the greenfinch's spring song?"

"Yes, I recollect," said the Doctor. "Sing it for us again, will you, please?"

"Certainly," said Pippinella, "I'll be glad to."

While the canary sang the beautiful and sad love story of the greenfinch, with the Doctor writing it all down in his notebook, the idea for a canary opera came to John Dolittle. It would be the most unusual dramatic production the world had ever seen, with Pippinella as the heroine and a cast of singing birds in the supporting roles. He determined to talk it over with her the moment her life story was finished.

The awed silence which greeted Pippinella at the end of her song convinced the Doctor more than ever that she was just the star he needed to take London by storm. Gub-Gub was sitting—silently, for a change—on his stool, with a big tear standing on the end of his nose. Dab-Dab was trying self-consciously to hide the emotion she was feeling at the conclusion of the song. And the other animals—Too-Too, Whitey, and Jip—were frankly wiping their eyes and snuffling their noses.

After a moment or two, while everyone composed himself again, the Doctor asked the canary to continue her story. Pippinella took another small sip of water and went on.

"At last our journey came to its end, as all journeys do, and we went ashore one fine morning and set about finding some means of transportation to get us to the town of the windmill.

"My friend's money was not yet exhausted, so happily we were able to pay for a coach ride. The window cleaner's anxiety and excitement about the fate of his book continued to grow as we drew nearer to his home. As we rumbled along over the country roads he kept muttering about the slowness of the horses and wondering aloud if the old mill had been burned to the ground or been struck by lightning or pulled down to make room for another building, and a hundred and one other possibilities that might prevent him from regaining his papers, even if his enemies had not stolen them.

"And when finally the coach set us down at an inn in the town where Aunt Rosie lived he took my cage beneath his arm and fairly ran along the road that led toward the mill. At the corner of the street he gave a cry, 'Thank goodness, Pip! It's still there. Look, the mill is all right. The next thing to see is whether the kitchen has been broken into.'

"And he ran stumbling on. The road up the hill was quite steep and he was all out of breath by the time he reached the little tumbledown fence that surrounded the bit of ground in which the mill tower stood. The place looked even more decayed and dilapidated than when we had seen it last. Long, lanky weeds grew in the chinks between the stones of the front walk. The little gate by which we entered hung by a single hinge.

"But the thing that struck us both was the fact that the front door of the mill had boards nailed across it.

" 'Humph!' I heard him mutter. 'The old farmer's been around and found the door letting the weather in.'

"Then he went to that side of the tower where the kitchen window was. And that, too, had been nailed up.

" 'Looks as though we're going to have a job to get in,

Pip,' said he. 'I think I'll set you down here while I run over to the outhouse and find a ladder. That second-story window seems about the only entrance—unless I break in. You wait here. I won't be a minute.'

"And he set my cage down on an old packing case near the front door and ran off toward the outhouse."

Pippinella paused.

"It's funny," she said presently, "what odd things happen at odd places. At that moment I was just as excited as he to know the fate of his papers. But when he disappeared into that outhouse, that was the last I ever saw of him."

"Why, what happened?" asked Gub-Gub. "Was he kidnapped again?"

"No," said Pippinella, "but I was. While I listened to him rummaging around in that old shed, searching for a ladder, I saw a ragged person, very evidently a tramp, creep out from behind the tower. His appearance at once made me suspicious. And I started to call for the window cleaner at the top of my voice. But I suppose the noise that he was making himself prevented him from hearing anything else. The tramp, with a glance over his shoulder, drew nearer. I hoped my friend would show up again any minute, for I knew at once what was going to happen. But he didn't. He was evidently entirely absorbed in his hunt for the ladder. As I gave an extra loud scream the tramp whipped my cage up, thrust it under his coat to muffle the sound of my voice, tiptoed out of the gate, and set off quickly down the hill.

"It would be quite impossible to describe to you how I felt. After all my striving, after all my traveling, there on the very doorstep of the mill, within a few moments of knowing what had happened to the book, within earshot of my beloved friend to whom I had only just been reunited, to be stolen by a tramp while his back was turned!

"He fell in with a caravan of Gypsies"

Fortune has dealt me some bitter blows, but none quite as bad as that.

"I think he was some kind of a Gypsy. And later he fell in with a caravan of Gypsies, who seemed to know him, and traveled part of the way with them.

"I guessed at once that he had not stolen me because he was fond of birds. His idea was to sell me. He had lifted me up and taken me along just as he would a knife or any other bit of movable property, when the owner wasn't looking. And now he just awaited an opportunity to dispose of me for money.

"And for two weeks I shared his wandering, hand-to-mouth existence. Often I was hungry; often I was cold; often I was wet. Still, I saw a tremendous lot of the countryside, and when the weather was fair I felt that I might easily be worse off, so far as the mere comforts of life were concerned.

"I tried to mark the way, to notice the road we followed, so that in case an opportunity to escape should occur I would know how to come back. But the course of his journey was too meandering to keep track of it for long. I calculated at the end of ten days that we had covered a hundred and fifty miles or so. But how much it would be in a straight line I had no idea.

"At one place my tramp nearly got caught picking a farmer's pocket at a cattle show. And I thought perhaps my chance to escape was at hand when the crowd started to come after him. But he was a wily rascal. He gave them the slip and got away.

"The tramp had tried several times to sell me at fairs and at wayside houses that he had passed. And, for my part, I hoped he would succeed. But somehow he didn't. Perhaps people had an uncomfortable feeling that he might have stolen me—for certainly he looked like a very suspicious sort of character.

"Anyway, after a while I saw what I feared most would probably come to pass—he would sell me at a bird shop. One early morning he made his way into a small town and, with my cage under his arm, presented himself at an animal store just as the doors were being opened and the place swept out. My heart sank as we entered. The smell and the noise and the crowding! Oh, my! They are still a sort of nightmare to me. I yet clung to the hope as we went in that the proprietor wouldn't buy me or would offer a price so low that the tramp would keep me. For, naturally, villain though he was, his open, wandering life through the countryside was better by far than the close quarters of that noisome establishment.

"But, alas! He was apparently desperately in need of a few pence, and while he struck as good a bargain as he could, he was evidently determined to sell me this time for anything he could get. And after a little haggling, he left me on the counter, took his money, and went away.

"And then began what was, I think—after my experience of the coal mine—the unhappiest chapter in my life's story. Why should I tell you all the drab details of that miserable existence? You probably know them already, and for my part, I hate to recall them. An animal shop! Heaven preserve all animals from sinking to that dreary state. There's no reason, of course, why these places shouldn't be run properly—so far as the cage birds are concerned, at all events. But the fact remains that they very seldom are. I found that all my parents had told me about them was true —and a good deal more in this case.

"The main trouble is the crowding. No one person—nor two people—can look after a couple of hundred birds, several dozen rabbits, six pairs of guinea pigs, four tanks of goldfish, a score of dogs, cases upon cases of pigeons, ten parrots, a monkey or two, white mice, squirrels, ferrets, and heaven only knows what more, and give proper attention to them all. Yet this is what they try to do. It isn't that they want to be unkind. They are just careless—horribly careless. They want to make money. That's the main idea.

"Right off from the start I was taken out of my little wooden cage, where I had lived since I'd been aboard ship, and pushed into a larger one that was crowded with other crossbred canaries. We stood on a shelf, one in a long line of cages, and over us and under us and all around us there were more cages still. My partners who shared my miserable box were a motley crew of half-moulted hens, some of them with sore feet, others with colds in the head—hardly one of them a decent full-blooded member of society. In the middle of the room parrots on stands screeched and squawked all day long. Twice a day—but why go on? There is only one good thing that I can say about that animal shop, John Dolittle: it was there that I first heard about you from the other poor creatures who shared my miserable fate; and it was there that you found me and rescued me from an existence too horrible to describe further."

"My, my!" said the Doctor. "A most dramatic turn of events! Just right for an opera."

"Opera?" screamed Gub-Gub. "You mean we're going to do an opera? How elegant. I shall sing the baritone's role —Figaro! Figaro! Figaro-Figaro-*Figaro!*"

"Oh, be quiet!" scolded Dab-Dab. "Nobody said we were going to do an opera. You're always jumping to conclusions."

"The Doctor said Pip's life was just right for an opera," said Gub-Gub crossly. "That's what you said, John Dolittle, didn't you?"

"Yes, I did," replied the Doctor. "But the opera I have in mind is for birds only. You—and the rest of the family— may help with the production. That is, if Pippinella is willing."

Then the Doctor outlined his plan to the canary and asked her if she would be willing to assume the leading role. He explained that he would use the exact story of her life for the plot and hire other birds to play the supporting roles. It was just the idea he had been hunting for, he told

HUGH LOFTING

"In the middle of the room parrots on stands
screeched and squawked all day long"

her, and he felt sure London audiences would be charmed
by such a production.

"Thank you, John Dolittle," Pippinella said. "It is a very
great compliment. I hope you won't be disappointed in me.
I shall need a great deal of coaching—opera is another
thing again from singing just for the pleasure of it. But I
have a small favor to ask of you, Doctor."

"Anything, Pippinella," said the Doctor. "What is it?"

"John Dolittle," replied the canary. "I want you to find my friend the window cleaner. If we go up to London, as you planned, we may just find some trace of him there."

"It is little enough to ask," said the Doctor. "And London will be a good place to start. We have many friends there. Cheapside, the London sparrow, who makes his home on St. Paul's Cathedral, can give us some valuable help, I'm sure."

Gub-Gub bounced down off his stool and, grabbing Dab-Dab around the middle, began to waltz her around and around, singing, "We're off to London to see the Queen! Tra-la-la-la, la-la-la, la-la!"

"Oh, stop it!" cried Dab-Dab. "You're making me dizzy!" But she was smiling just the same and joined in the jubilation with the others.

PART THREE

· The First Chapter ·

THE CANARY OPERA

THE DOLITTLE caravan and circus started immediately for London and set up camp on Greenheath outside the city limits. Cheapside was found, and helped the Doctor and Matthew Mugg, the cat's-meat man, with the gathering together of birds from private aviaries, the zoo, and from the open fields. Theodosia, Matthew's wife, took over the making of all the costumes for the opera while the Doctor and the cat's-meat man attended to the details of production.

When it came time for rehearsals to begin they still had not found a suitable bird to play opposite Pippinella—to sing the tenor role.

"We need a voice that will blend perfectly with hers," said John Dolittle to Matthew. "It's important that he be of good appearance, too."

Before Matthew could reply Pippinella, who was listening from her cage nearby, called out, "Why don't we try to find Twink—the mate I had when I was with Aunt Rosie?"

"Oh, Lor' bless us, Pip!" cried Matthew Mugg. "It'd be like tryin' to find a needle in an 'aystack."

"Let's not give up until we've had a look around," said the Doctor. "It may be possible to find Twink."

With Pippinella going along to help, Matthew visited every animal shop in the vicinity of London. Strangely enough, one day in a dirty East End store, who should turn up but Twink. He was desperately ill with a cold and a sore throat but the Doctor soon fixed that with his Canary Cough Mixture, and Twink's voice came back stronger and more beautiful than it had been before. Pippinella was delighted to see him again and, for the time being, stopped fretting about her friend, the window cleaner.

Twink's account of the miserable conditions under which the birds and animals existed in the East End shop so disturbed the Doctor that he and Matthew took time out from rehearsals to stage one of the greatest mass rescues in the Doctor's career—the release of Twink's former associates from their imprisonment in the shop.

In spite of the fact that the Doctor often neglected the business of the opera to follow up some clue that seemed to be leading to the window cleaner, Pippinella's beloved master was still not found. One day, when the Doctor had called a final dress rehearsal, it was discovered that the green canary and Jip were missing. Cheapside, who was assisting the Doctor by drilling the chorus and dance numbers, was all for finding a new prima donna.

"Temperamental hartists!" sniffed the cockney sparrow. "I bet them two is off 'untin' for 'er window polisher. Say, Doc, what's the matter with me singin' 'er part? We could dye my feathers green and nobody'd know the difference."

"Hah!" snorted Dab-Dab. "If you so much as opened your cockney mouth the audience would clear the house in two minutes!"

"I like that!" replied Cheapside in a huff. "I'm considered the most musical bird in these 'ere parts, I am!"

"Now, now," admonished the Doctor. "Pippinella must be found. We can hold up opening for a day or two. I'm sure she can't be far away."

And Pippinella *was* found. She explained that she had seen a man in the circus enclosure who looked like her window-cleaner friend. Jip had gone with her to follow him across London. But in the smelly quarters of the docks even Jip's sensitive nose could not keep track of the scent.

The Doctor was most understanding.

"I know how much you miss him, Pippinella," he said. "But do be patient. As soon as the opera is over we will devote every minute to make a thorough search for him. Please promise me you won't run off again."

"All right, Doctor," replied the canary. "I'll wait."

The Canary Opera was a smashing success. Pippinella's solos, "Maids, Come Out; the Coach Is Here," "The Harness Jingle," and "The Midget Mascot," were tremendous hits. She was so taken up with the excitement of being the toast of London that, for the time being, thoughts of her friend, the window cleaner, were completely driven from her mind.

Many honors, too, came to the green canary because of the opera. She was wined and dined at the most famous restaurants in London. Admirers sent her baskets and bouquets of flowers; and a famous manufacturer of birdcages paid her a large salary to hop in and out of one of his cages in a store window, showing by her presence and sprightly manner that she approved of the design.

The successful opera season came to a close. Twink went off to live with Hop, the clown from the circus, who had decided to retire. The pelicans and flamingos had been returned to the naturalist from whom the Doctor had borrowed them for the chorus, and the thrushes and wrens had left for their native haunts. All that was left to do now, before the family could return to Puddleby while the Doctor and Pippinella went to look for the canary's friend, was for the circus animals and personnel to be placed in proper homes for their comfort and well-being.

This the Doctor did with great care. He chartered a special ship to send the lion, the leopard, and the elephant back to Africa. The snakes went along too and caused great consternation when they got out of the basket on the dock and started diving and wiggling among the passengers' baggage just for the fun of a good stretch. One old lady fainted dead away when she opened her bag for inspection and saw one of them squirming among her shawls and laces.

However, they were captured and made the trip safely and happily back to their native soil, where they became the talk of all snakedom with the fandango dance that they had learned for the circus and now performed for their newfound friends.

The day finally came when all the business of the circus had been completed. The enclosure was cleared of its equipment; nothing remained now except the Doctor's caravan—in which members of his household lived—and the smaller covered wagon which served Theodosia and Matthew Mugg as a home.

A vast throng of children—after presenting the Doctor with a huge bouquet of flowers—were departing tearfully sucking on peppermint candies John Dolittle had given them as a farewell present. The Doctor turned to face the members of his family who were gathered around him.

"I—a—er, have something to tell you," he said. He paused, at a loss for the proper words.

Dab-Dab, quick to sense what was in the Doctor's mind, pushed forward to stand in front of him.

"Now, John Dolittle," she said crossly. "Don't tell me we are not going home. I simply cannot stand another minute of this Gypsy existence! My nerves are at the breaking point!"

"There, there," said John Dolittle leaning forward to comfort her. "I know it's been difficult. But you've done a wonderful job. And I wouldn't even consider keeping you here. How soon will you be able to leave?"

"Why, within the hour!" said Dab-Dab, brightening. "I have one or two little things still to do." She spread her wings and, calling to the others to come and pick up their rubbish, flew right through the doorway of the wagon. Matthew and Theodosia also hustled off to complete their preparations while the Doctor just stood in the empty lot staring off into space.

Barely a moment elapsed before Dab-Dab thrust her head out of the wagon and looked at the Doctor with a worried expression on her kindly face.

"I just remembered something, Doctor," said the duck. "You didn't say what it was you had to tell us."

"Why, I—er—a—you see, Dab-Dab," he began.

"Don't tell me—I know," she said, coming slowly down the wagon steps. "You're not going to Puddleby with us. I might have guessed it. You have some notion of finding that window-cleaner fellow, haven't you, John Dolittle?"

"Yes," said the Doctor. "I made a promise and it must be fulfilled before I can return to Puddleby."

"All right!" declared Dab-Dab. "If that's the way you feel, then nobody goes to Puddleby until you do."

"Oh, that isn't necessary, Dab-Dab," remonstrated the Doctor. "Perhaps the others *want* to go home."

With that there was a chorus of denials; nobody wanted to go home without the Doctor.

"We can all help find Pip's friend!" shouted Gub-Gub. "I'm a first-class rooter!"

"Where do you think he's hiding?" asked the duck, all thoughts of Puddleby driven from her head. "Under a cauliflower plant?"

"Jip will be better at hunting him out than any of us," said the white mouse. "He can track a person by sniffing the grass along the roadside."

"Whitey would be valuable wherever doors are locked," offered Jip. "He can squeeze through a hole the size of a farthing."

"How about me?" asked Too-Too the owl. "We may need to do some night work. And you know how well I see in the dark."

Pippinella, perched on a discarded orange crate, listened to all this with a lifting heart. During the earlier proceedings she had become terribly downcast, for she too had mistaken the Doctor's intentions. But when she heard with what enthusiasm the family accepted the change in plans she flew to the group and lit on the Doctor's hat.

"I want you to know how much I appreciate this," she said in a most gracious manner. "Someday, perhaps, I can do something for you besides upsetting your plans."

"Tut, tut," said Dab-Dab, who was secretly a great admirer of the little prima donna. "We frequently change our plans. Don't we, Doctor?"

"Yes, indeed," said John Dolittle. "Now let's work out the beginning of our campaign. Pippinella, do you know the name of the town where the windmill stood? That seems the best place for us to start."

"Yes," replied the canary. "It's called Wendlemere, a little town with a cathedral right in the middle and a river that makes a sort of loop around three sides of it."

"The cathedral stands at one end of a large market square, doesn't it?" asked the Doctor.

"Yes," said Pippinella. "That's the town."

"Fine," said the Doctor. "Now we're on the trail. Did you ever hear your friend's name?"

"Never once," said the canary. "He was careful always to avoid giving any name. And as I told you, so far as his life at the mill was concerned, no one was ever around to ask it."

"Humph!" said the Doctor. "It isn't much to go on, just the name of the town. Still, people have been found before today with no more information than that. I will do my best. Now, let's all go back to the caravan for supper. Dab-Dab, have we something extra nice? Some kippers and tea would taste good after this busy day."

"Kippers!" squealed Gub-Gub. "I'd rather have a kipper than a dozen truffles!"

During supper a lively discussion went on; everybody wanted to go along to hunt for the window cleaner. But it was finally decided that only Jip and Pippinella should accompany the Doctor. Matthew and Theodosia were commissioned to see that Dab-Dab had sufficient food for the larder at all times; and the family all joined with Pippinella in making plans for the trip to the windmill.

In the morning the Doctor, Pippinella, and Jip were up and away early. It took them the whole day to complete the journey to Wendlemere, and by the time they got there darkness had fallen.

"I'm going to have a look around," said the Doctor. "One can tell better at night if a place is occupied—by the lights in the windows, you know."

"Smells are good at night too," said Jip. "The dampness makes them hang close to the ground. I'll go along, if you don't mind, Doctor?"

"Certainly, Jip," said the Doctor. "Pippinella, you come onto my shoulder. We'll stroll around and see what we can see."

The little party set out for the mill while the rest of the town slept. They went immediately to the foot of the hill on which the windmill stood, to see if any light were visible in the tower. But all was in darkness.

"Perhaps he's gone to bed," said the canary hopefully. "It's long after midnight. And he used to turn in early when we lived here before."

"Yes," said the Doctor, "and I think that's what we better do too. We'll find a room at the inn and wait until morning to investigate further."

On the morrow they returned after a hasty breakfast to the home of the solitary philosopher. Their first glance at the mill from below the hill was quite discouraging. No smoke rose from the stovepipe that stuck out of the roof. Yet it was the hour when breakfast, if the mill were occupied, should be cooking. With a sinking feeling of failure, the Doctor, with Pippinella on his shoulder and Jip at his heels, hurried up the hill till finally he stood before the little gate in the ramshackle fence. The stone walk leading to the tower door showed no footprints of habitation.

Heavy at heart, the Doctor turned his head to speak to Pippinella.

"We've come on a wild-goose chase, Pippinella," he said. "Your friend, evidently, has been gone from here a long time."

"I'm afraid you're right, Doctor," said the canary. "What do we do now?"

Jip jumped up and put his paws on the Doctor's leg.

"There's a man over there in the field," said he. "Why don't you ask him if he's seen the window cleaner?"

"That's a good idea, Jip," said the Doctor. "Perhaps he

"He stood before the little gate in the ramshackle fence"

owns this place. He'd be sure to know something about his tenant if he did."

The man, a weather-beaten, gray-haired countryman of about fifty years of age, turned out to be a civil fellow—only too willing to rest his plow and gossip, if he got the chance.

"No," he said. "I ain't seen nowt of that queer loon for—let me see—not for over a year. He used to pay me a few shillings a month for the use of the old mill. He'd bring me the money regular himself, while he was here. Didn't like to have me come up and collect it. It seemed he hadn't no wish for human company around him. I never even heard what his business was."

Suddenly the man peered sharply at Pippinella sitting on the Doctor's shoulder.

"That's queer, Sir," he said. "That fellow you're lookin' for had a bird the spittin' image of that one. Used to hang his cage on a hook outside the tower window—when the weather was good. But of course, it couldn't be the same one. Yours seems sorta tame-like—the way he sits there—not moving or nothing."

The Doctor was relieved that the man did not pursue the subject further; it would be awkward to try to explain his relationship with birds and animals to this simple countryman.

"He wur surely a strange, strange man," the farmer went on. "I used to say to the wife, I'd say, Maybe he's a hanarchist, a-mixing dynamite and bombs up there in my mill—never did see a soul live so secret and solitary. Oh, go along, she'd say, no man with a face like his'n never mixed bombs to blow folks up with. He looks more to me like a minister—and not any of your simpering psalm-singing kind neither, but just a plain, honest man who thinks more of others than himself. That wur the wife's opinion. Howsomever, hanarchist or minister, he wur a queer duck, all right."

"Do you remember exactly," the Doctor asked, "what day it was you saw him last?"

The farmer called to his team to stand and he scratched his head.

"Aye," he said, after a moment. "I mind it wur the day I took the potatoes in off the north field. It rained about noon, and I had to stop 'cause potatoes don't store good

" 'He wur surely a strange, strange man,' the farmer said"

when they're wet. I hadn't even seen him go away. But his
not coming with the rent told me that he'd gone off and I'd
like as not never see him again. Then, when I were starting
for home I saw a man a-crossin' down from the mill to the
gate. It wur him. He wur running, crazy-like. So, I thinks
to meself, He's come back, 'as he? Minding he never like to
have me come to see him, I thinks to meself: He'll be
around to my place afore long with his rent and I'll not
bother. And I goes off home in the rain. But he never

comed and I never seen him from the fields here while I was plowing. And at the end of the week I goes up to the mill, anyhow. But he wasn't there."

"Yes, but what day was that?" asked the Doctor.

"It wur the day I took the potatoes off the north field," the farmer repeated, "end of the first week in September. That'll be twelve months ago come Friday."

"And have you seen anyone else around the mill, either before or since?"

"Not a soul. Nobody ever comes up here."

"Thank you," said the Doctor. And bidding the farmer good-bye he set off to return to the town.

· The Second Chapter ·
THE GREEN PARROT HAS A CLUE

WHEN John Dolittle got back to the inn he put Pippinella back in the small traveling cage he had made for her.

"There's plenty of seed and fresh water, I believe," he said. "You must be very hungry."

"No, Doctor," said the canary. "I'm too discouraged to eat."

"You mustn't feel that way," said the Doctor. "We've only begun to look for your friend. I feel sure he'll turn up. Have some food—and rest a while. I'm going out to ask around the town whether a stranger has been seen lately. Jip, you stay here to keep Pippinella company. Try to cheer her up while I'm gone."

Jip wagged his tail and said he would.

At a corner of a long street of stately old-fashioned mansions the Doctor paused a moment, looking upward at a curious lamppost that stood close to one of the houses. Two fine shade trees spread their branches overhead. Outside the corner window of the house a mirror was fastened on a bracket. A plump, white-haired lady sat knitting at the window, and the Doctor noticed that she was looking at him in the mirror. Something about the spot struck John Dolittle as familiar. And while he paused an old lame man came along, put a ladder against the lamppost, and climbed up to clean the lamp.

A smile of recognition suddenly spread over the Doctor's face.

"Aunt Rosie's house!" he whispered. "Of course. I wonder if she's heard anything of the window cleaner. There she is, still knitting, still watching the neighbors pass. I'll go and call on her."

Aunt Rosie, while knitting at her window, had noticed a small, round man pause at the corner of the street.

"Hah! A stranger!" she muttered, dropping a stitch. "Distinguished-looking man. A scientist or a barrister—possibly a diplomat. I wonder what house he's bound for. Doesn't look like a relative of anyone in this street. Goodness gracious, I believe he's coming here! Yes, he's walking up my steps. Well, did you ever! Emily!"

A maid, neatly dressed with white cap and apron, entered from the next room in answer to her mistress's cry.

"Emily," said Aunt Rosie, "there's a caller at the door—a gentleman caller. I'm not dressed or anything. Get me my cashmere shawl quickly. It's on the top of my bureau. And take this old woolen one away. There's the bell. Hurry! I've no idea who it is, but it looks like someone very important. He's got a black bag. Come from out of town, that's clear. Are the tea things ready? Answer the door, girl. Don't stand there like a dummy! No, get the shawl first. And don't forget the buttered toast. Hurry, I tell you! Here, come back. Put this old woolen thing out of sight."

In a great state of flutter and excitement Aunt Rosie threw off the white knitted shawl from her shoulders—nearly upsetting a green parrot that perched on a stand at her elbow. The maid, bewildered at receiving half a dozen orders at once, took it from her and left the room. In the hall she set it down upon a chair and went to open the front door.

Without she found a small, round man, with a very kind face.

"Er—er, hum—er—a. Is Aunt Rosie in?" asked the Doctor.

The maid stared at him in astonishment.

"She is, I know," the Doctor went on, answering his own question. "Because I saw her at the window."

Emily, though still somewhat at sea, found her voice.

"Won't you come in, sir?" she murmured.

"Thank you," said the Doctor, stepping across the threshold.

In the hall on his way to the parlor the Doctor was met by the hostess herself, who came forward, fluttering, to greet him.

"Ah, how do you do, Aunt Rosie?" said he, holding out his hand.

Now "Aunt Rosie" was a nickname for this lady, used only by herself when talking with her pets and some of her relatives. Imagine, then, her astonishment to be greeted in this fashion by a complete stranger. However, her guest seemed such an amiable, disarming person, she supposed he must be someone whom she ought to know and whose face she had forgotten.

"Good afternoon," she murmured feebly. "Emily, take this gentleman's hat and bag."

Then she led the way into the room where she always sat, and the first thing the Doctor noticed was the green parrot perched on the stand.

"Ah!" said he. "I see you've got a new parrot. The other one was a gray one, wasn't he?"

"Er—yes. Quite so," muttered Aunt Rosie, feeling surer

than ever that this man, if not one of her own relatives greatly altered, must at least be someone she ought to know extremely well. Afraid to offend him by asking him his name, she proceeded to potter around with the tea things while she watched the Doctor out of the corner of her eye and sought wildly to remember who he was.

Before the Doctor had a chance to explain the object of his visit he was offered, to his great delight, a cup of tea by his fluttering hostess.

"I hope you will pardon my dropping in unexpectedly like this," he began, taking a teacup from her.

"Oh, don't mention it," said she, returning to the tray. "Let me see, I've forgotten whether you take sugar?"

"Two lumps, please," said the Doctor.

"Yes, of course," murmured Aunt Rosie.

"Well, now," said John Dolittle, "I wanted to ask you about your window cleaner. You remember the odd fellow that you used to employ, the one you gave the canary to?"

"Oh, perfectly," the hostess answered, still cudgeling her brains for the name of this man who apparently knew her private affairs so well. "A quite extraordinary individual— most peculiar."

"Have you seen him recently?" asked the Doctor. "I mean since you gave up having your windows done regularly by him—that was somewhat over a year ago, wasn't it?"

"Yes," said Aunt Rosie, "I have."

For the quiet old lady of the sleepy cathedral town that odd character, the window cleaner, had always held the spice of mystery. Many a time she had tried by questioning him and inquiring among the neighbors to find out more about him. But she had met with nothing but baffling failure. The object of the Doctor's visit, therefore, threw Aunt Rosie into a greater state of excitement than ever. She

"She leaned forward in her chair"

stopped rattling the teacups and leaned forward in her chair as though about to impart some terrible secret.

"I had not seen that man," she whispered, "for fifteen months. I supposed that he had left the town, and I'm quite certain that he had, for several of my neighbors used to employ him, and if he had been working in the town I would surely have seen him. Well, then, one day, as I was feeding the parrot, I saw him come up the steps. I noticed at a glance that he was greatly changed, much thinner—he used to be quite plump, you know. And when the maid let him in, he asked for work. I didn't really need him to do the windows because I have them done by the maids now. But he looked so down-at-heel and poverty-stricken that I hadn't the heart to say no. So I told him to do all the windows on the top floor. On the way upstairs he suddenly swayed weakly against the wall. I guessed at once what was the matter. I whispered to the maid to take him to the kitchen and give him a good meal. And, do you know, the poor man was actually starving. The cook told me he ate nearly everything in the larder. Then I questioned him while he was at work, to see if I could find out what had befallen him. But he would tell me hardly anything. Just murmured something about having run into bad luck."

As Aunt Rosie finished her long speech the green parrot on the stand moved restlessly, jingling the chain about his leg.

"And did you, madam," asked the Doctor, "see him again after that?"

"Only once," said the old lady, handing her guest the buttered toast. "Seeing what sad straits he was in, I told him I wanted the rest of the windows done the following day. He came back early on the morrow—very early—and the maids told me they had seen him hanging around the house in the small hours. I believe he never went to bed at all; perhaps he had no place to go, but just waited through the night to do the rest of his work the following day. When all the windows were done and there was nothing further to keep him I asked him, as I paid him his money, whether he intended staying in the town for some time. He glanced at me suspiciously, as though I were trying to incriminate him, and then said no, he was remaining only long enough to make his coach fare to go on farther."

"Did he say where he was going?" the Doctor asked.

"No," said the old lady. "But I'm pretty sure he left the town that night. Because he finished his work here in the forenoon, and I never saw him again."

At this moment Emily, the maid, entered and whispered something in her mistress's ear.

"Excuse me," said Aunt Rosie, rising. "I have to see the butcher about his bill. I'll be back in a moment."

And she left the room, accompanied by the maid.

John Dolittle put down his teacup and leaned back in his chair, staring in a puzzled manner at the ceiling.

"Confound the luck!" he said aloud. "It looks as though the trail leads no farther. For heaven only knows where he went when he left the town."

Suddenly the Doctor heard a rattle behind him. Thinking it was perhaps his hostess returning, he sprang to his feet politely and turned about. But he found that he was still alone, except for the green parrot, whom he had forgotten. That wise-looking bird now seemed very wide-awake. He stepped gravely to the end of his short perch and craned his neck out toward the Doctor.

"Oh, how do you do?" said John Dolittle in parrot language. "You had been so quiet behind me there I had forgotten all about you. I suppose you can't help me in this problem?"

The parrot glanced over his shoulder at the door still ajar and listened a moment. Then he motioned with his head to the Doctor to come a little nearer. John Dolittle at once stepped up to his stand.

"He went to London, Doctor," the parrot whispered. "You know, as the old lady told you, he used to mutter a lot —talk aloud to himself—but only when there were no people around. While he was doing the window of this room, standing on the sill outside, with the sash half open, he looked in and saw me on my perch here. Seemed sort of mesmerized at first. Then he laughed kind of childish-like and went on polishing the window. There was no one in the room but me. 'Good old Pip,' he kept saying. 'There you are, still, sitting in the window. Watching me polish up the glass. So you came back to the old lady, did you, Pip? Well, she's a good sort. She'll take better care of you than I did. Poor old Pip! But you're looking well—you've grown bigger. Shan't see you again after today—not for a long time. I'm just making enough money to get after them, Pip. Curse them! Curse them! I'm just making enough money to buy a coach ride. Then I'm off. I know where they've gone, Pip. They've gone to London. And I'm going after them—tonight!' "

As the green parrot finished speaking the Doctor heard Aunt Rosie's footsteps in the distance, coming up the kitchen stairs.

"Listen," he whispered quickly, "did you get any idea of where he was going in London—any names of people he meant to see, eh?"

"No," said the parrot, "nothing more. I don't think he had a very clear idea himself. He seemed so sort of hazy. Tell me, Doctor, how is Polynesia getting on?"

"Oh, did you know my Polynesia?" asked John Dolittle.

"Why, certainly!" said the parrot. "She's a distant relative of mine. I heard that she was living at your house in Puddleby."

"I left Polynesia in Africa," sighed the Doctor, "last time I was there. I have missed her terribly."

"She's lucky," said the parrot. "She always was a lucky bird, was Polynesia. Look out, here comes the old lady back!"

When Aunt Rosie reentered the room she found her caller scratching the parrot's head.

"I'm sorry to have been so long," she said. "But you

know what these tradesmen are. That dreadful man insisted that I had two pounds of steak last Tuesday, when that is my meatless day. I haven't eaten meat on a Tuesday in three years—not since Dr. Matthews put me on a diet. Then he discovers that he sent the steak to somebody else on the street—someone who really had ordered it—and he had charged it to me by mistake."

"Very trying," said the Doctor. "Very trying."

Aunt Rosie now settled down again to her tea, hoping to find out from her caller something of the private history of her mysterious window cleaner. But before she had a chance to put a single question the Doctor began asking questions himself.

"Perhaps your maid—the one who opened the door for me—could remember something that would help me find the window cleaner," said the Doctor.

"Oh, Emily!" said Aunt Rosie, wrinkling up her nose. "She never notices really important things. But we'll ask her anyway."

Then Emily was summoned and questioned by her mistress. She said all she knew was that he hadn't done a very good job on the windows the last time he'd washed them. As she was retiring the front doorbell rang.

"Pardon me," said Aunt Rosie, rising. "This is my at-home day. Some friends drop in regularly and bring their needlework with them."

"Oh—er," said the Doctor, getting up out of his chair. "I think I ought to be going, really."

"Oh, no, don't run away," said Aunt Rosie. "I'll just see who it is. I'll be back in a moment."

And before the Doctor had a chance to protest, his hostess had left the room again and closed the door behind her.

HUGH LOFTING

"Then Emily was summoned and questioned by her mistress"

In the hall Aunt Rosie greeted a sour-faced lady who had just been admitted by the maid.

"My dear," she said, fluttering forward, "I'm so glad you've come. Listen, there's a man in the parlor whom I can't make out at all. He seems to know all about me and my private affairs. And I suppose it's someone whom I ought to know extremely well. Perhaps you can help me. If you recognize him, whisper his name to me when he's not looking, will you?"

"Is that his?" asked the sour-faced lady, sternly pointing to the Doctor's hat hanging on the stand in the hall.

"Yes," said Aunt Rosie.

"Then I know already," said the other.

Now, as soon as Aunt Rosie had left the parlor the Doctor was summoned by a sharp "Pst!" from the corner of the room. He slipped across to the parrot's side and leaned down to listen.

"It's your sister, Sarah," whispered the bird. "She's always the first to arrive at these sewing circles. They're all a dreadful lot of old gossips, but she's the worst of them all. A sparrow told me that she's your sister."

"Good heavens!" said the Doctor. "Sarah! How can I get out of here, I wonder?"

"Push the window up and drop down into the street," said the parrot.

"But my hat and bag are in the hall," whispered the Doctor. "I can't go without them. Oh, Lord! And she'll start in about the circus again, I suppose, as soon as she meets me."

"Listen," whispered the parrot. "You see that other door over there? That leads around through the pantry. Go through it and wait just on the other side. As soon as they come in here and the hall is clear I'll give a loud squawk. Then hurry along the passage and it will bring you out into the hall. Take your hat and bag, and let yourself out of the front door. Hurry up! I hear them coming."

The Doctor only just closed the door behind him as Sarah and Aunt Rosie entered the room. He waited a moment in the narrow dark passage till a hearty screech from the parrot told him that the coast was clear. Then he groped his way along till he found the door at the end, passed into the hall, grabbed his hat and bag, and let himself out onto the street.

"Dear me!" he muttered as he hurried around the corner and set off toward the inn. "A lucky escape, a merciful escape! I don't know what poor Aunt Rosie will think of me, running off like that. Well, well! I haven't found out an awful lot about the window cleaner. Still, it's a good deal to know that he's in London. It's an awfully big city, though. But you can't tell. I have a feeling that we'll run him to earth yet."

· The Third Chapter ·
CHEAPSIDE HELPS THE DOCTOR

THE DOCTOR went immediately to his room at the inn and told Pippinella the result of his expedition. When he had ended the canary shook her head.

"It looks bad," she said, "—very bad, Doctor. From what both the farmer and Aunt Rosie told you, there is no doubt in my mind that the window cleaner found his kitchen ransacked and his papers gone. Oh, dear! Poor man. I suppose he was just distracted with grief. What can we do, Doctor? What can we do?"

"Well, now," said John Dolittle, "be patient. After all, it's something that we know he went to London. I have a kind of a notion that we're going to succeed in finding him."

"Oh, I hope so," sighed Pippinella. "I hope so. I'm so worried about him."

"I hope we don't end up down at the East End docks again," said Jip. "I simply can't get the smells untangled. What with tar smells mixing with the scents from boxes of spices the ships from India unload on the docks, and the fish smells so strong one can barely breathe, I find it impossible to pick out the man smell."

"Yes," said the Doctor. "It must be very difficult. Let's hope we don't have to go there."

That evening the little party took the London coach from the town square. As there were no other passengers for that trip the Doctor was able to stretch out on one seat and sleep most of the way. When they reached the city it was early morning and everything was bustling with activity. The Doctor tucked Pippinella's little traveling cage under his arm so that in case they should meet the window cleaner among the crowds on the streets the canary could recognize him. Jip trotted along at John Dolittle's heels, ready for action.

As they walked along the thronged pavements Pippinella with her keen eyes searched the faces of every passerby hoping to find her friend. After about two hours of this they all began to be a bit tired. On his way across a bridge that spanned the river, the Doctor sat down on one of the public seats to take a rest.

"Dear me, Doctor," said the canary. "I'm afraid there isn't much chance of our running into him haphazardly. Look at those crowds across the bridge! Their faces all swim together when I try to pick out one at a time."

The Doctor, who was beginning to be pressed about the prospect himself, did not answer. Presently he arose and moved off, with the intention of finding Cheapside, the London sparrow who had promised to help them find the window cleaner.

Passing by St. Paul's Cathedral he looked up at the statue of St. Edmund which stood against the sky. The Doctor knew that Cheapside and Becky, his wife, made their nest in the ear of the great statue. And although he couldn't see it from that distance, he hoped it was there and that Cheapside would be home and would see him.

Suddenly he saw a small speck shoot out of the statue's

" 'Lor' bless me, Doc!' said Cheapside"

ear. It dropped to earth with the speed of a bullet and, with a fluttering of wings, landed on his shoulder.

"Lor' bless me, Doc!" said Cheapside. "I 'ad no idear you was in town. When I looked down off St. Edmund's ear just now and see'd your old stovepipe 'at, you could 'ave knocked me over with a feather!"

"Well, well, Cheapside," said the Doctor. "I'm glad I found you so easily."

"But what are you doin' 'ere, Doctor?" asked the

sparrow. "When I went out to Greenheath yesterday they told me you was in Wendlemere—'untin' for Pip's friend."

"We were," replied the Doctor. "But we had no luck. Nobody there has seen him for months and months. However, I did hear that he'd come up to London. Then I remembered that you had promised to help us, and we came to find you."

"So I did," said Cheapside. "So I did. And I ain't one to go back on my word. I'll do my best. London's a big place. Still, there ain't no one knows it better than what I do. Hello, Pip," he said, peering into the cage under the Doctor's arm. " 'Ow's the primer donner this morning?"

"Very well, thank you," said Pippinella. "But I'm terribly worried about my friend."

"Don't you fret now, Pip," said the sparrow. "We'll find the bloke if we 'ave to 'unt the whole of England over. Just you leave it to old Cheapside. I'm the champion 'unter of the British Hempire, I am! You and the Doc and Jip—hello Jip," he said. "I was so busy talkin' I forgot to say hello."

The sparrow hopped over onto the Doctor's other shoulder.

"As I was sayin'," continued the sparrow, "you three go back 'ome and wait to 'ear from me. I'll bring you word as soon as I 'ave something interesting to tell you."

"I'm awfully glad we found him," said John Dolittle as they made their way homeward toward Greenheath. "He'll be much better at tracing your friend than I could ever hope to be. You see, he's lived in London all his life—knows every street and house in the whole city."

"I do hope he finds him," sighed Pippinella. "But I'm very fearful. Suppose those spies have found him again and taken him off on that dreadful ship."

"Now, now, Pippinella," said the Doctor. "We mustn't look on the dark side. I still feel confident he's around someplace. Let's leave it to Cheapside for a while. If it's possible to find him he'll do it. He'll do anything for me."

Reaching Greenheath, the Doctor was met by Gub-Gub and the rest of the family clamoring for news of the window cleaner.

About noon the next day, when the Dolittle household was sitting down to lunch in the wagon, two sparrows suddenly flew in at the open door and settled in the middle of the table—Mr. and Mrs. Cheapside.

As soon as the greetings were over Dab-Dab provided them with a place beside the white mouse (next to the salt cellar) and gave them a supply of crumbs and millet seed.

"Bless me, Doctor," said Cheapside with his mouth full. "It's nice to sit down to dinner with you again. Becky and me 'ave been kinda lonesome for you since the opera closed."

"It's nice of you to say so," replied the Doctor. "We've missed you, too."

"Ah, Doc," said Cheapside. But he was secretly very pleased.

"By the way, Cheapside," said the Doctor. "I don't want to seem impatient, but have you started your search for Pippinella's friend yet?"

"Who's that?" asked the sparrow.

"The window cleaner—you know," said the Doctor, "the man I spoke to you about yesterday."

"Oh, 'im?" said the sparrow. "Yes, we found 'im all right."

"You found him!" cried the Doctor, springing to his feet. "Already? Good heavens!"

"Yes," said Cheapside. "We ran 'im down this morning— about eleven o'clock."

A regular chorus of exclamations broke out around the

Doctor's luncheon table after Cheapside's extraordinary statement.

"When will he come here?" asked Gub-Gub, climbing up onto his chair to make himself heard. "I'm so anxious to see that window cleaner."

"How was he looking?" asked Pippinella.

"Whereabouts did you find him?" Dab-Dab wanted to know.

"But, Cheapside," said the Doctor. "How on earth did you do it in so short a time?"

"Well," said the sparrow when the general noise and clatter had quieted down, "the first thing I did was to go 'round to the gangs."

"What do you mean, the gangs?" squeaked the white mouse.

"The sparrow gangs, of course," said Cheapside. "The city sparrows are divided into gangs. Very exclusive, some of them, too. F'rinstance, the West-Enders; oh, my! They're lah-di-dah, they are! Live in Cavendish Square, Park Lane, and Belgravia. Call 'emselves the Four Thousand—gentry, you know. They wouldn't be seen speakin' to a Whitechapel sparrow or any of the Wapping gang, Mile-Enders, Houndsditchers, and low bird-life like that. Hoh, no, indeed! Then there's the sort of betwixt-and-betweeners—the Chelsea push, live among the artists; the Highgate and Hampstead lot, 'ang around among the writers, they do. They're kind of 'alf-and-'alf, sort of dingy—you know, down-at-'eel genteel—look glum on Sundays, never do their fightin' on the street, all for keepin' up appearances. But they're all the same to me, see. Whitechapel, Highgate, or Belgravia—I don't take no lip from none of them.

"Well, when you says you wants to find this window washer of yours, I says to the missus, I says, 'Becky, the Doc wants this bloke found. It's up to us to run 'im down.

You go 'round the 'igh-life gangs'—you see, she uses better-class talk than what I do—'and I'll go 'round the East-Enders and the middle-class 'ippocrites. I'll meet you on top of Cleopatra's Needle at ten o'clock sharp. Tell the gang leaders the job is for the Doctor and I'll want to know the reason why if it ain't done right. If that bloomin' window swabber ain't located by noon, the feathers'll begin to fly—and they won't be mine, neither.'

"So Becky goes off one way and I goes off another. The first bunch I hinvestigates is the Greenwich squad. They 'ang 'round the docks, all the way from the Tower to the Isle of Dogs. I looks up the leader right away, One-Eyed Alf, they calls 'im—the Wapping Terror. Thinks 'imself a fighter. I 'ad to push 'is 'ead in the gutter before I could make him listen to reason. 'Hark at me, you crumb-snatchin' stevedore,' I says, ''ave there been any strangers come 'round your district lately?'

" '' Ow should I know?' 'e says off-'and like. 'I ain't the Lord Mayor!'

" 'Well, look 'ere,' I says, 'you get busy with your boys and bloomin' well find out, see? There's a window cleaner missin' and the Doctor wants 'im found. Your gang of pickpockets will know if any new faces have settled in the Greenwich District. I'll be back this way in 'alf an hour. And I'll hexpect reports, see! Now, 'op about it, you moth-eaten son of a dishrag!'

"It's no use mincin' words with that Greenwich lot. A kick behind the ear is the only hargument they understand. Well, then, I goes off up the river for Chelsea, to set the next gang to work.

"Inside of 'alf an hour," Cheapside continued, "I'd got around all the gangs in my 'alf of London. And I felt pretty sure that if your friend had settled anywhere within their boundaries I'd get to 'ear of it, all right, because, you'd be surprised, there's nothing that escapes the eye of a city sparrow. You could ask any bird in the Piccadilly Circus gang at what hour any of the theaters close up, and they could tell you to a minute. You see, they get their living picking up the scraps of cake that the ushers sweep out when the audiences go 'ome. The Westminster lot could tell you the name of any member of Parliament that you might see going or coming out of the 'Ouse of Commons. The St. James Park lot could tell you what the queen 'ad for breakfast and whether the royal babies slept well last night. We go everywhere. We see everything. Yes, when it comes to city news there ain't nothing we don't know.

"Well, to return to where we was on my way back to Cleopatra's Needle to keep my appointment with Becky 'ere, I drops in again on One-Eyed Alf, to see what news 'e 'ad for me. 'E told me as 'ow 'e tracked down three or four window washers, new arrivals, in his district. But not one of them answered the description I'd given 'im. You remember Pippinella 'ad told me that 'er man 'ad a scar across the side of 'is 'ead where the 'air didn't grow no more. And, although several of Alf's gang had spent hours 'angin' 'round sundry window cleaners at work, waiting for them to take their 'ats off to scratch their 'eads, they 'adn't seen one with a scar like what your canary 'ad described."

"But he might not be working at window cleaning at all now," said Pippinella. "That wasn't his real profession."

"Yes, I know. But we found 'im, anyway," said Cheapside, "as you will 'ear. And it came about through that scar you told me of, too. I questioned Alf for a few minutes and I come to the conclusion as 'ow 'e 'ad covered the ground thorough. So I scratches Greenwich and the Lower River off the list and goes on to meet Becky.

"Becky told me," Cheapside went on, "that she 'asn't

been able to find out nothing. 'It's queer, Beck,' I says, 'very queer.' Then she says to me, she says, 'Maybe the man's sick'—you know you'd spoken of his being unwell—'and if 'e is sick,' says Becky, ' 'e'd not be seen by the ordinary sparrows. Better get the 'ospital birds on the job.'

" 'Right you are,' I says. And off we both goes to look up the 'ospitals. There's quite a lot of them in London, you know. But with the 'elp of some gang leaders we goes around them all. When we'd come to the last of 'em and still 'adn't 'eard nothing I say to the missus, I says, 'Becky, it looks as though we'd got to go back to the Doctor with empty 'ands.'

" 'It's a shame,' she says. 'And 'im trustin' us, and all.'

"And then, just as we was movin' off to come 'ere, up flies One-Eyed Alf, the Wapping Terror.

" 'We've found 'im,' 'e says, short-like.

" 'You 'ave?' I says. 'Where is 'e?'

" ' 'E's in the Work'ouse Infirmary,' 'e says, 'over in Billingsgate.'

" 'You're sure it's 'im?' says Becky.

" 'Yes,' says 'e. 'Not a doubt of it. Come over and take a look at 'im, if you don't believe me.'

"Then we flies off with Alf and 'e takes us to a dingy sort of place in Billingsgate, next to a glue factory. It's a sort of an institution for the destitute. Old men and women and folks that ain't got no 'ome is took in there. And those what are able-bodied 'as to work, and those what ain't walks around in a yard with 'igh walls. Kind of a cheerless place.

" 'Come over 'ere,' says Alf, leading us off to the north end of the yard. 'This is the infirmary, where they keeps the sick ones, that yellow brick building with all the windows in it.'

"We follows 'im and 'e flies along a line of windows, lookin' in as 'e passes, and at the fifth one 'e stops and we lights beside 'im on the sill. Inside we sees a bed and a man's 'ead a-lyin' on the pillow. Across the side of 'is 'ead was a scar. I goes close up to the glass, and presently the man rolls 'is 'ead from side to side and starts talking to 'isself. 'Pippinella,' he cries. 'Where are you? They've opened the 'ole in the floor, and the papers are gone.'

"What 'e meant I don't know. But as soon as I 'eard 'im call the canary's name, I knew we'd run the right man down at last.

" 'Come on,' says Becky. 'That's 'im, all right. Let's go and tell the Doctor, quick.' And 'ere we are."

The sparrow had hardly finished speaking before the Doctor had risen from his chair and was reaching for his hat.

"Thank you, Cheapside," said he. "We are both ever so grateful to you. If you and your wife have finished lunch we will go down there at once, and you can show us the way. Did you mark the room, so I can inquire for the right bed? We don't even know the man's name."

"I couldn't tell you what the inside of the infirmary is like, Doc," said Cheapside. "But you can locate 'im, all right, because I saw a card 'ung up on the foot of 'is bed and on it was written a number—No. 17."

"Can't I come with you, Doctor?" asked Gub-Gub, as John Dolittle hurried toward the door of the wagon.

"I'm sorry, Gub-Gub," said the Doctor. "But I'm afraid it won't be possible. You see, I'm going to a hospital."

"But I don't mind going to a hospital," said Gub-Gub.

"No, quite so," said John Dolittle. "But—er—I'm a little afraid they may not let me in if I brought too many pets. They're sometimes rather fussy in hospitals."

Gub-Gub was very disappointed, but the Doctor had to be quite firm because he was really afraid that he might

" 'Can't I come with you, Doctor?' asked Gub-Gub"

not be admitted himself if he took the pig with him. Jip, too, had to be left at home for the same reason. Finally John Dolittle set out with Pippinella and Mr. and Mrs. Cheapside for London.

· The Fourth Chapter ·
JOHN DOLITTLE, M.D.

JOHN DOLITTLE hadn't been in London more than five minutes before he discovered news of his arrival had already spread among the animal life of the city. This, of course, was due to the gossip of Cheapside and his fellow sparrows of the streets. While the Doctor and his party were still at the station where they had just stepped down from the Greenheath coach, a funny, scrubby little bird flew up and whispered something to Cheapside, who was traveling with the Doctor. Cheapside brought him forward and introduced him.

"This is One-Eyed Alf, Doctor," said Cheapside, "the feller I was telling you about. 'E's got something 'e wants to say to you."

"Oh, how do you do?" said John Dolittle. "I'm very glad to make your acquaintance. I learn that it was largely through you that we have been able to locate our man. We are very grateful to you."

The newcomer was indeed a strange-looking bird. The first thing the Doctor noticed about him was that, in spite of his having only one eye, he seemed very alert and wide-awake. He had several feathers missing from his tail and altogether looked like a very rough customer.

"Don't mention it, Doc," said he. "Only too glad to be of any 'elp. O' course, I'd 'eard a whole lot about you, and we city folks are always 'appy when you pays us a visit. I got a sister over in Wapping what got herself tangled up in a clothesline. I'd be glad if you could come and take a look at her. She's broke a wing, I think. Ain't been able to fly none for over a month. We've 'ad to bring 'er crumbs to 'er and feed 'er like a baby."

"I'll certainly do anything I can," said the Doctor. "Take us to where she is, and I'll see what can be done."

"Look here, Cheapside," whispered Pippinella as the party set off in a new direction under the guidance of One-Eyed Alf, "you'll have to protect the Doctor. Once it gets 'round that he is doctoring animals he is just swamped with patients of all kinds. Dab-Dab told me it always happens this way. He'll never get to my window cleaner if you let him be sidetracked by every sparrow who wants to see him."

And it turned out that Pippinella was right in her fears. For when John Dolittle arrived at the place where One-Eyed Alf was leading them, he found plenty of work ready for him. In the backyard of an empty house in one of London's slummiest quarters there was awaiting him not one sparrow but more than fifty. Birds with broken legs, birds that had been bitten by dogs, birds that had fallen into paint pots—even birds that had their tails injured under carriage wheels were there. All the accidents, all the casualties of London's sparrowdom were gathered to await the arrival of the famous Doctor.

"I'm sorry, Doc," said One-Eyed Alf as he gazed over the collection of patients waiting in the grimy yard. "I didn't mean to let you in for nothing like this. I told Maria to keep quiet about your coming 'ere. But you know 'ow women is—they must talk."

"Lor' bless us!" murmured Cheapside, scratching the top of his head with a thoughtful claw. "Like Puddleby days, ain't it, Doctor? I don't know what you better do. I s'pose the dogs and cats will 'ear of it next, and you'll 'ave another bunch of hinvalids waitin' for you tomorrow. P'raps you better disguise yourself and let me give it out that you've left town."

"No, Cheapside," said the Doctor. "That would never do. I must patch these birds up, now I'm here. But I think you had better let it be known that I will see animal patients between seven and ten every morning out at Greenheath. That's what I've had to do in other towns—regular dispensary hours. Now, which is your sister, Alf?"

"That's Maria across there in the corner," said the gang leader. "Hey, Maria! Come over 'ere. The Doctor wants you."

A very dejected little bird, trailing a stiff wing behind her on the ground, shuffled her way through the throng of sparrows and approached the Doctor.

In a moment John Dolittle had his little black bag open, and then his fat but nimble fingers got busy with the tiny wing joints of the patient.

"Yes," he said, "it's broken—in the upper bone. But we can fix it, all right. You'll have to wear a cast for a week or two and carry your wing in a sling. Find a dry sheltered spot, a place where cats can't reach you, and keep perfectly still for ten days at least. Have your brother, Alf, bring your meals to you as before. Don't peck this plaster off till I have seen you again. There you are, now! A strip of this handkerchief will make a sling for you—so—around your neck. Now you're all fixed up. Next, please."

The second patient to come forward was a very woeful sight—a young, inexperienced bird who had been fighting on a new building. In his excitement he had fallen into a paint pot and all his feathers were caked stiff with white lead, making it, of course, impossible for him to fly. The Doctor's task here was to take the paint out of the plumage without injuring the bird's skin.

The afternoon was more than half gone before the Doctor had attended to all his patients and was able to continue his journey to the workhouse.

Reaching that rather gloomy building at last, he knocked upon the door marked Visitors and was admitted by a porter. He had asked Cheapside and Becky to wait for him outside. He was conducted to a large waiting room and presently the superintendent appeared and inquired whom it was he wished to see. When he said it was someone in the infirmary, the doctor in charge was brought forward. Not knowing the window cleaner's name, John Dolittle had to describe him as best he could, and at length he succeeded in making the authorities understand who it was.

"Oh, you mean the man in bed No. 17?" said the doctor in charge. "Humph! You can't see him. He's very sick."

"What's the matter with him?" asked John Dolittle.

"Memory gone," said the other, shaking his head gravely. "A very bad case."

Well, finally, after explaining that he himself was a doctor of medicine, the visitor was told that he might see the sick man, but must not remain with him long.

"He gets so easily excited," the workhouse doctor explained as he led the way down a long passage and up a flight of stairs. "We moved him into a private room last week. It's a very mysterious case altogether. He seems to

" 'You can't see him' "

have forgotten even his name. Gets dreadfully worked up when anyone asks him. I'm afraid we have very little hope of his recovery."

Upstairs they were taken to a small room at the end of another corridor. And by the light of a candle, for it was now growing dark, the Doctor saw a man lying in a bed.

"He seems to be sleeping," John Dolittle whispered to the doctor in charge. "Would you please leave me with him till he wakes up?"

"All right," said the other. "But don't stay long, and *please* don't get him excited."

As soon as the door was closed the Doctor brought Pippinella's cage out of his pocket and stood it on the table beside the bed.

"It's he, Doctor," whispered the canary. And she chirruped gently with joy. Instantly the man on the bed opened his eyes and tried weakly to sit up. For a moment he stared stupidly at the bird in the cage.

"Pip-Pippin—" he began hesitatingly. "No, I can't remember. It's all hazy."

"Pippinella—your canary. Don't you recognize her?" said the Doctor quietly from the chair beside the bed.

The sick man had not realized there was another person in the room. He turned suddenly and glared at the Doctor in a funny, frightened sort of way.

"Who are you?" he asked suspiciously.

"My name is Dolittle," said the Doctor, "John Dolittle. I'm a physician. Don't be afraid of me. I've brought you your canary—Pippinella."

."I don't know you," said the window cleaner in a hoarse gasp. "This is some plot—a trick. But it's no good now. You can't worm any secrets out of me. I haven't any. Don't even know my own name. Hah! It's a good joke. Everything a blank. Memory gone. And no one can get it back for me. I was so successful keeping my life a secret from the world that now no one can tell me even who I am!"

As the window cleaner finished speaking he sank back on the bed and closed his eyes.

"Oh, dear!" whispered Pippinella. "What shall we do, Doctor? What shall we do?"

The Doctor thought a moment in silence. Then he leaned forward and touched the patient gently on the shoulder.

"Listen," he said. "Please believe that I am your friend. I

don't want to trick you into telling me your secrets. I know a great deal of your life already. In fact, I am the only man in the world who does know. You have been very ill. But you are going to get all right again. You are going to get your memory back. Let us see if we can't recall things. You remember the windmill on the hill?"

Very quietly and soothingly John Dolittle then told the window cleaner the story of his own life, which he had learned through his knowledge of bird language from Pippinella. At first the man on the bed listened without a great deal of attention. On and on the Doctor went, telling of the old cathedral town, of Aunt Rosie's house, of the secret writings, of the kidnapping, the escape from the ship, of Ebony Island, the raft, the rescue. Gradually the window cleaner's haggard face showed interest. At length, when the Doctor was describing his return to the mill and his finding the place deserted, the patient suddenly gave a cry and clutched John Dolittle by the arm.

"Stop!" he cried. "I remember now. The old windmill—the hole in the floor where I kept my papers. Did you steal them?"

"No," said the Doctor quietly. "I have told you I am your friend."

"But how do you know all this?" cried the other. "It's all true—every word. It's coming back to me. Tell me what you are."

"I'm just a doctor," said John Dolittle, "a doctor who has spent most of his life learning the ways and the speech of animals. Most people think I'm crazy when I tell them that. But it's true. You see the canary on the table there?"

"Yes," said the window cleaner. "That's Pippinella. She was stolen from me when I got back to the mill."

"Exactly," said the Doctor. "Well, it was she who told me the story of your life. If you don't believe me, give me

" 'I'm just a doctor,' said John Dolittle"

some question now to ask her, and I'll show you that I can do as I say."

The sick man gazed at the Doctor a moment, still with something of suspicion in his eyes.

"Either you are crazy or I am," he said at last.

"I know," said the Doctor, smiling. "That's what everybody says. But give me a question to ask and I'll prove it."

"Ask her," said the window cleaner, "where I kept the ink."

And then he chuckled to himself quietly.

The Doctor turned and exchanged a few words with the canary at his elbow.

"She tells me," said he, facing the bed again, "that you never used ink at all. You wrote in indelible pencil—everything. Is that right? She says you kept a box of them on the kitchen mantelpiece."

The window cleaner's eyes grew wide with wonder.

"It's uncanny," he murmured, "—absolutely uncanny. And yet—what you say *must* be true. The things you've told me, about the journey back to the mill—and all the rest—there was no one there but her, Pippinella. Funny I always thought she was listening and watching. So you speak her language, eh? It sounds impossible. But it must be true. I—I am sorry if I mistrusted you."

When the infirmary doctor reentered the room John Dolittle at once broached the subject of the patient's being moved as soon as possible. This apparently meant a great deal of filling out of papers and signing of documents. The Doctor had to guarantee that he would care for the sick man for a certain length of time. That of course he was quite willing to do. And after a day had been agreed upon for his next visit, he and Pippinella left and set off on their way home.

The canary's joy knew no bounds. She was a different bird. She sang all the way home. The night air was cold; so the Doctor put her little traveling cage in his pocket. But even there, so great was her relief to know that her friend the window cleaner was safe, she went on warbling away at the top of her voice. And people passing the Doctor in the street were entirely puzzled to know where the sound was coming from.

When the Doctor and Pippinella arrived at Greenheath

"The whole family gathered about him"

the whole family gathered about him as soon as he entered the wagon, clamoring for news.

"When is he coming?" cried Gub-Gub.

"Next Thursday," said the Doctor, "if he is well enough to make the journey. I think he will recover more quickly here than at the infirmary. Theodosia, do you think you could fix up a bed in your wagon for Pippinella's friend? He'll need a great deal of rest at first."

"Certainly, Doctor," said Theodosia. "I'll be happy to."

That night Pippinella entertained the whole company with her gayest songs. She was in splendid voice because the window cleaner was found, and she would have gone on all night if Dab-Dab hadn't brought the celebration to an end by reminding them that it was past twelve o'clock and time they were all asleep.

· The Fifth Chapter ·

THE WINDOW CLEANER
TELLS HIS NAME

THURSDAY came, the day when the Doctor had said he would bring Pippinella's friend away from the hospital if he was well enough to travel. And the devoted canary had the poor Doctor out of his bed very early that morning, you may be sure. Indeed, it was barely light when John Dolittle, driving a hired wagon so as to have plenty of space to carry Pippinella's friend comfortably, set out with Matthew Mugg for Billingsgate.

On their arrival Matthew took charge of the horses at the door while the Doctor went in to see the patient.

He found the window cleaner greatly improved and most anxious to leave and come with him. And as soon as some more forms had been filled out and signed, the sick man was helped into the waiting vehicle and they started back for Greenheath.

On the way the Doctor discovered now that the window cleaner had recovered his memory he was most anxious to get on the trail of his lost papers again. It was quite clear too that whatever suspicions he had had about John Dolittle's honesty, he now trusted him completely.

HUGH LOFTING

"The canary had the Doctor out of his bed very early"

"And is it your intention," the Doctor asked, "to go on with your writing as soon as you are able?"

"Why, certainly," said the other. "But of course I must first get some sort of a job by which I can earn enough money for living expenses."

The window cleaner was half sitting, half lying in the covered wagon. The Doctor was seated beside him. Matthew was up in front driving.

"Humph!" murmured the Doctor. "Er—by the way, I

never learned your name. Of course, if you don't want to tell me, it is your business and you have a perfect right to keep it to yourself. But while you are with us it would be more convenient if we have some name to call you by."

The sick man sat forward slightly to see if Matthew was listening. Then he turned to the Doctor again.

"I trust you," he said. "I am—or was—the Duke of Loughborough."

"Great heavens!" said the Doctor. "But who then is this man who now holds the title? The day we arrived in London I noticed in the papers that he was leaving town for the north."

"That is my younger brother," said the window cleaner. "When I disappeared he came into the estate and the title. They supposed I was dead—as I intended they should."

"Well, well!" murmured the Doctor. "Tell me, why did you do it?"

"It was impossible for me to write the way I wished, freely, while I was still a duke. I would have gotten my government, my friends into trouble."

"I see," said John Dolittle. "And have you never regretted disappearing? Have you never wished to go back to your dukedom?"

"No," said the other firmly, "never! I may often have been sorry that I had no money to do the things I wished. But I've never regretted the step I took."

"I understand," said the Doctor. "Well, now listen, we must have some sort of a name to call you by while you are with us. Have you any preference?"

"Call me Stephen," said the window cleaner.

"Very good," said the Doctor. "Ah, look, we're coming to Greenheath now. Matthew and Mrs. Mugg have made room for you in their wagon; and make yourself entirely at home. And, please, ask for anything you want."

On their arrival at the now deserted circus enclosure the Doctor insisted on the window cleaner going to bed at once and remaining there until he gave him permission to get up. His meals were given to him by Theodosia, and he was treated like one of the family.

So great was Gub-Gub's interest that the pig sneaked around secretly to get a glimpse of the window cleaner from behind Mrs. Mugg's skirts when she brought his lunch to him. And after he had learned that he was a real duke he could scarcely be kept away from the neighborhood of the Muggs's wagon.

"You know, I always suspected," he said at supper that evening, "that he was some great person in disguise. I suppose he used to ride in a carriage and drink out of gold basins before he became a window cleaner. Fancy giving up all that just to be able to write!"

"He gave it up for the sake of the poor people he would help by his writing," said Too-Too.

"It's a good thing, Doctor," Dab-Dab put in, "that you are the only one who can understand animals' language. Otherwise the man's secret would be all over the country now that pig knows it."

"How long will he stay with us, Doctor?" asked Jip.

"I'm not sure yet," said John Dolittle. "Certainly till he is well enough to get around by himself. For the present he undoubtedly needs constant medical attention. He has not taken care of himself at all. That's one reason why his condition is so low."

"But after he gets well," asked Jip, "is he going back to the mill?"

"I haven't discussed that with him," said the Doctor. "He says he will need some kind of a job—just to make enough money to carry on with."

Pippinella, who had been listening to the Doctor's family

"He sneaked around secretly to get a glimpse of him
from behind Mrs. Mugg's skirts"

discuss her friend, came forward and said, "I won't hear of
him going to work, Doctor. I have plenty of money saved
up from the opera. He took care of me; now I'm going to
take care of him."

"Well, Pippinella," said the Doctor. "You can put it to no
better use, I'm sure. In the meantime, he shall stay with us
as long as he wishes."

Within a day or two after Steve joined the Doctor's

family, John Dolittle noticed that he did not seem as contented as he might be. Not that he said anything or complained. On the contrary, he frequently spoke gratefully of how fortunate it had been for him that he made the Doctor's acquaintance. But he so often seemed wrapped in thought and moody.

"He's thinking of those papers he lost, Doctor," said the canary one evening after supper when they were discussing Steve. "His health is much better, and he's getting stronger all the time. But that is what is making him unhappy. In the evenings he lies in bed with a pad on his knees and tries to write; but always it ends the same way. 'What's the use,' he mutters. 'Even if I could remember the book and rewrite it word for word—which I couldn't— even then I wouldn't have the documents to prove what I say.' Then he falls to mumbling and cursing the men who robbed him."

"Humph, too bad! Too bad!" murmured the Doctor. "I wonder if there's anything I could do. Let me see, I might go back to the mill with him. But I doubt even then if I could do much."

"Well, try it anyway, Doctor," Pippinella pleaded. "You never can tell."

"All right," said John Dolittle. "If he wants me to go with him we'll take a run up one day soon. I'm sure he's well enough now. We'll take Jip with us."

Dab-Dab, who had been listening to the Doctor and Pippinella, fluttered her wings with annoyance.

"John Dolittle!" she demanded noisily. "You said that as soon as you found Pippinella's friend we would go back to Puddleby. Well, now he's found. Why must we wait around this deserted old mud hole?"

"Dab-Dab," said the Doctor. "I'm just as anxious as you to get home. But neither Pippinella nor Steve will be really happy until we at least make an effort to find the missing papers. I'm sorry, Puddleby will have to wait."

"Oh, bother!" snapped the duck. "The trouble with you, John Dolittle, is that you never think of yourself."

Whitey, who was curled up half asleep in the Doctor's pocket, stuck his head out and said, "Listen who's talking, Doctor. Why, Dab-Dab spends every minute of every day doing something for others."

"Quite so, Whitey," said John Dolittle, smiling.

The following morning, after the Doctor had examined Steve thoroughly, he told him that he could get up now and spend part of each day in the sunshine. But the good news didn't raise the window cleaner's spirits as it should have. He obeyed the Doctor but sat dejectedly on the wagon steps staring into space. Then the Doctor asked him if he would like to run up to Wendlemere soon and look around the mill. Steve jumped at the offer with such enthusiasm that even Dab-Dab was glad they were going to have a try at locating the lost papers.

And that is how John Dolittle came to make still another trip to Aunt Rosie's town—this time accompanied by the window cleaner himself. Dab-Dab packed a lunch for the two men—with a bone for Jip and seed for Pippinella. They took the morning coach from Greenheath with the canary in her cage and Jip under the seat.

· The Sixth Chapter ·

THE SEARCH FOR
THE MISSING PAPERS

THE PARTY reached its destination late in the evening and, after spending the night at the inn, proceeded the next morning to the mill. Things here were, of course, in a more dilapidated condition than before. But it surprised the Doctor somewhat to find the door to the kitchen unlocked and a great litter of nut shells and fruit stalks and other rubbish about the floors and windowsills. This he at first supposed must have been left by rats or squirrels. But of these creatures themselves—or, indeed, of any animal life—nothing could be seen. Hanging from a beam on the ceiling were two bats fast asleep.

In the center of the kitchen floor was the hole where Steve had kept his papers. Beside it lay the big stone that had covered it, just as he had left it when, after discovering that his property had gone, he had departed, determined to proceed to London.

In bringing Jip along the Doctor had hoped that his keen sense of smell and his eye for tracks might help in the search. And they were hardly inside the door when Jip put his nose down in the hole and sniffed long and noisily.

"Well," asked the Doctor, "what about it, Jip?"

For a moment Jip did not answer but continued sniffing

"Jip put his nose down in the hole"

and snuffling at the hole in the floor. Then he smelled the stone that had been the lid, or cover, to the hole. Finally, he looked up at the Doctor and said, "The scents are mostly quite old ones and therefore very faint. It's curious the strongest of them is a badger—but not in the room here, only in the hole."

"How odd!" said the Doctor. "Badgers don't usually have much to do with buildings. But how about the scent of men? That's there, too, isn't it?"

"Yes," said Jip, "surely. But it is very dim. Of course I can plainly smell your friend the window cleaner. The scent of his hands on the stone is fairly distinct still. But other men have been in the room around the hole quite a while before, and some again since Steve was here, I should judge. That's what puzzles me so. It would seem as though there had been two lots of men here—at different times. And then on top of it all the smell of this old badger is so strong that I'm surprised the other scents are not drowned out entirely. It is a very difficult problem in smelling altogether."

"Humph!" muttered Steve gloomily, though of course he had not understood what Jip said. "I'm afraid I've brought you on a fool's errand, Doctor. Everything is pretty much as I left it. You can see for yourself that the hole is empty."

"What did he say, Doctor?" asked Jip. "I didn't quite get that."

"He is discouraged," said John Dolittle. "He fears that there isn't much chance of our doing anything."

"Well, don't let him go away yet," said Jip. "I haven't finished by any means.

"There's some sort of mystery here," Jip continued. "It's funny how different those two lots of men smelled. The first lot had a sort of office smell—parchment, sealing wax and ink and all that sort of thing. Probably there were two in the party. And the other was an open-air man—smelled of wood fires, stables, the mud of roads, and rank tobacco. Oh, look out! Don't disturb that hole, Doctor!"

John Dolittle had knelt down and was feeling around in the loose earth that lay at the bottom of the hole.

"Why, Jip?" he asked, rising.

"You'll get the smells all mixed," said the dog. "Let's just leave it exactly as we found it. It'll be much easier to pick up a scent so. The first thing we've got to do is to try and run down that old badger. While you're going over the mill on the inside to see if you can find out anything, I'll make a circle outside around the hill and try to pick up that badger's trail. I have a kind of notion that if we can only get hold of him he'll be able to tell us a whole lot."

"Why?" asked the Doctor.

"Well—I've a kind of notion," said the dog.

Jip, who, as you know, was quite a wonder at the fine arts of smelling and tracking, dearly loved to wrap a certain amount of mystery around his doings when employed on work of this kind. The Doctor was always willing to humor him in this and never insisted on an answer if the great expert seemed unwilling to give one. So this morning he just drew Steve off and set about examining the house and left Jip to his own devices.

All this time Pippinella was tucked away in her little traveling cage in the Doctor's pocket; she had kept absolutely quiet as she didn't want to be a bother to them. But she was relieved when John Dolittle put his hand in his pocket and drew her out.

"My goodness, Pippinella," said the Doctor anxiously. "I'd forgotten all about you. I *am* sorry."

"That's all right, Doctor," said the canary, blinking at the unaccustomed light. "Perhaps if you let me out I could be of some help to you and Jip."

"Certainly," said John Dolittle, releasing the catch on the cage door. "But don't go too far away from us. We may have to run for it, and we don't want to leave you behind."

"I'll be careful," said Pippinella. "I'll just ride around on Steve's shoulder—if you don't mind."

"Not at all," said the Doctor. "Your place is with him."

Of course the window cleaner could not understand the conversation between the Doctor and Pippinella, but he smiled and stroked her head when she flew onto his shoulder.

"Good old Pip," said he. "It's like old times to see you there."

The Doctor with Steve then made a very thorough examination of the premises both inside and out. They discovered very little, however, beyond what appeared to be signs that the mill had been occupied not so very long ago. There were still bits of candle ends here and there, some moldy apple peels, a needle and thread, which the window cleaner was quite sure he had not left behind.

These, of course, might have showed nothing more than that the farmer had let the mill again to some other person since Steve had left. But both the Doctor and Steve thought it wiser not to go and ask him.

In the meantime the hour for lunch arrived and the Doctor sat down with his companion to enjoy the meal Dab-Dab had prepared for them. And still Jip had not returned. Indeed, it got to be four o'clock in the afternoon before he showed up. And when he did he looked anything but satisfied with the results of his expedition.

"It does beat everything," he sighed as he flopped down wearily on the kitchen floor, "how far a badger can travel when he makes up his mind to move quarters. Holy smoke! Since I last saw you, Doctor, I've covered a circle a good twenty miles across, but not a vestige of that long-snouted old vagabond could I find. I struck many a trail, dozens—none of them very fresh—but I followed each one to the bitter end, just to make sure. They all wound up the same—at the old hole that Mr. Badger had rented out to the beetles a month or so before I got there. Then I consulted all the farm dogs within miles. Most of them knew him—said he was a funny, cunning dodger. They'd never been able to catch him, though every one of them had tried many times. They reckoned it was about two or three months since he had disappeared. And that's all I got for one of the heaviest day's work ever put in."

"Maybe some of the dogs killed him—ones whom you didn't talk with," said the Doctor. "Or possibly he may have died of old age. Badgers don't live terribly long, you know."

"No," said Jip patiently. "I hardly think that's worth taking into account. This fellow was not an old badger and, from what I hear, he should have been easily able to take care of himself against dogs. And, as for traps, well, you know how farm dogs get around. They nose into every corner of the countryside and find out everything; they say there just aren't any traps set in these parts. And there you are."

"Humph!" said the Doctor. "And you couldn't find any other badgers?"

"Not a one," muttered Jip.

The Doctor gazed through the dirty, cobwebby kitchen window for a moment, thoughtfully watching the setting sun that reddened the sky in the west.

"How about the rats and the mice in this place?" Pippinella asked. "There used to be plenty of them when we lived here. Maybe they could tell us something."

"That's what I was thinking as I came back across the fields," said Jip. "But I don't suppose the duffers will know. They never know anything useful. But we might try. You'll have to do it, of course. They're scared to death of me. I'd better get outside so they won't smell me so strong."

"All right," said the Doctor. "I'll see what I can do."

And then, as soon as Jip had disappeared, the Duke of Loughborough, otherwise known as Steve, was treated to the spectacle of John Dolittle summoning his friends the rats. Standing in the center of the kitchen floor, the great naturalist suddenly screwed up his face and squeaked in an extraordinarily high voice, at the same time gently scratching the wood of the tabletop with his fingernails. Then he sat down in the chair and waited.

After five minutes had passed and nothing had happened, the Doctor went to another part of the room and repeated his peculiar summons. But still neither rats nor mice appeared.

"That's very extraordinary," said John Dolittle. "I wonder why they don't come. A place like this, unoccupied, must be simply riddled with rats."

Just as he was about to go through his performance for a third time Jip scratched at the door and the Doctor let him in.

"It's no use," the dog said. "You can save yourself the trouble, Doctor. There are no rats here."

"None here!" cried the Doctor. "Why, that's hardly possible. I should have said this was an absolutely ideal home for rats and mice."

"No," said Jip. "There isn't a one. I've been around the outside, examining the place where the holes come up into the open air. I know the looks of a hole that's occupied. Even without smelling it I can tell whether it's in use or not. And I didn't find a single one that rats had passed through in weeks."

"Well," said the Doctor. "I'm not going to doubt the opinion of an old ratter like you, Jip. But it's most extraordinary. I wonder what's the reason for it."

"Poison," said Jip shortly, "rat poison. Lucky for me they used a kind I know the smell of. I picked up a bone around the back of the mill. And I was just going to start chewing it up when I caught a sniff that made me drop it like a red-

HUGH LOFTING

"The Doctor let him in"

hot poker. I've been laid up once by eating meat that had been poisoned and set out for rats to nibble. And I'll never get caught again. I was so sick for two weeks I could scarcely move. Well, to go back, after I'd dropped the bone I started to nose around the outhouses, and I came across some bits of stale bread that had more poison smeared on them. Then I found one or two dead rats in the ditch a little distance away. That's the reason that there are none in the house. Someone poisoned them all off. And, if you ask me, I should say it was a pretty experienced rat-catcher."

"Well, but they'd come back," said the Doctor, "if this work was done some time ago—as it surely must have been. Other rats would have come to live here, even if all the old ones had been killed off. There's no one living in the place now to keep it clear of them."

Jip came up close to the Doctor and whispered in a mysterious manner, "I'm not so sure."

"What do you mean?" asked John Dolittle.

"I'm not so sure there isn't someone living here—right now," Jip whispered. "I told you there was something mighty queer about this place. I saw signs around the doors of those outhouses that makes me almost believe that someone is making his home here."

"Great heavens!" muttered the Doctor. "This is uncanny. But if someone was living here, even in hiding, you'd have smelled him surely, wouldn't you? Your nose would have led you right to the place where he's concealed."

"It would," growled Jip, "if it wasn't for that blessed old badger. The trails are so crossed and the scents so mixed up no dog could follow a smell here without getting led off it after two or three yards. Wait! Did you hear that sound?"

"No," said the Doctor. "Where was it coming from? My goodness, how dark it's getting. The sun has dropped below the hill. I had no idea it was so late. No, I didn't hear any sound," the Doctor repeated.

"I thought I did," said Jip, "a sort of fluttering noise. But maybe I was mistaken."

"Listen, Jip," said John Dolittle. "If what you suspect is true, and there is someone living here, we had better set to work to find him. I don't think it's possible, myself. But your suspicions are so often correct. Now, let's see, what

"They got an old ramshackle ladder and climbed into the attic"

places are there where a man could hide? There's that old attic over our heads; there are the outhouses. And that's about all, isn't it? Oh, what about a cellar? No, there can't be any cellar because that hole in the floor has earth in it, and if there were a cellar beneath we could see right down into it. No, the attic in the tower and the outhouses are the only places we need bother with. All right? Let's set to work."

And after the Doctor had explained Jip's suspicions to

Steve, they got an old ramshackle ladder and climbed into the attic. Jip stayed below to watch and help, should they discover anyone there, and Pippinella went along with the Doctor and Steve.

"Hang on tightly to Steve's shoulder, Pippinella," said the Doctor. "We mustn't get separated in the dark."

· The Seventh Chapter ·
THE SECRET HIDING PLACE

HE ATTIC of the old mill was filled with every conceivable kind of rubbish. Bundles of old newspapers were piled on top of broken furniture; cobwebs had gathered on dilapidated trunks and boxes; and discarded clothing lay in heaps of dust and dirt, their threads chewed and crumbled by a hundred generations of moths and beetles.

"It's obvious no one has been up here for a long time," said the Doctor, lighting another match. "This dust hasn't been disturbed since these things were put here."

However, the Doctor crawled around on his hands and knees and peered into every corner. When they came down, and after the Doctor had taken a candle out of his little black bag (for now they could barely see a foot ahead of them, the night was so black), they went around to the back of the mill to examine the outhouses.

Here they had no better success. The ruined buildings contained nothing more than junk, lumber, and odd parts of mill machinery.

"Humph!" muttered the Doctor as they started back for the kitchen. "I think you must be mistaken, Jip—although, goodness knows, you very seldom are in these funny notions of yours. If we could find some life in the place, rats, mice, squirrels—any kind of animals—I could question them and get some information. Listen, Steve, you are sure there is no cellar to the place?"

"There was none when I was here," said Steve. "Of that I'm sure."

On reaching the kitchen they found it quite dark inside. For more light the Doctor was about to open his bag and get a second candle when he discovered to his astonishment that it was no longer on the table.

"That's curious!" he muttered. "I could have sworn I left the bag on the table."

"So could I," said Jip. "But look, there it is on the chair."

"And it has been opened," said the Doctor, going toward it. "I'm certain that I latched it when I left the kitchen."

The Doctor opened the bag and looked inside.

"Why, somebody's been through it!" he whispered in astonishment. "Everything's here, all right. But it's all topsy-turvy inside. *It has been searched while we were out!*"

For a moment the Doctor and the dog gazed at one another in silence. Finally John Dolittle whispered, "You're right, Jip. There's someone in the house. But where?"

Slowly the Doctor looked around the walls.

"If only I could find some animal life," he muttered.

"Sh!" said Jip. "Listen!"

All four of them kept still. And presently, faintly but quite plainly, they heard a curious little fluttering, rustling sound.

"Look!" said Jip, pointing his sharp nose up at the ceiling. "The bats! They're just waking up with the coming of dark."

The Doctor looked up. And there, from a beam across the ceiling, hung two little bats. Fitfully and sleepily they stirred their wings, making ready to start out on their night rounds. They were the only living things that John Dolittle had seen since he had entered the mill.

"Dear me!" he said. "Why didn't I think of that before? Bats—of course! Nobody could poison them off without first poisoning the flies. Well, I must see what they can tell us."

The odd furry creatures were now circling around the room, their queer shapes throwing strange shadows on the wall in the dim light of the candle.

"Listen," said the Doctor in bat language (it was a very strange language and consisted mostly of high needle-like squeaks, so faint that they could scarcely be heard by the ordinary ear). "I have several things I would like to ask you. First of all, is this house occupied?"

"Oh, yes," said the bats, still flying around in endless circles. "Someone has been living here off and on for ever so long."

"Is there anyone here now?" asked the Doctor.

"Most likely," said they. "He was here last night. But, of course, during the daytime we sleep. He may have gone away."

"What can you tell me about this hole?" asked the Doctor, pointing to the floor.

"That was where the man beside you kept his papers," said the bats.

"Yes, I know that," said John Dolittle. "But the papers were stolen or something during his absence. Did you see anything of that?"

"It was a very complicated, mixed-up business," squeaked the bats. "But, as it happened, we saw it all because, although the papers changed hands three times, it all took place in the evening or night, and we were awake and watching."

HUGH LOFTING

"The odd creatures were now circling around the room"

"The papers changed hands three times!" cried the Doctor. "Good heavens! Go on, go on! Who took them first?"

"The badger," said the bats. "He used to live outside, but he thought he'd like to come inside for the winter. So he started making a tunnel from the outside. We watched him. He bored right down and came up in the middle of the floor. But the flagging stones were too heavy for him to lift and he could get no farther. However, one evening a man came around and made his home here.

"Then about a week afterward two more men came. The man who was living here hid himself. The two newcomers hunted and hunted as though they were looking for something. At last they started taking up the stones of the floor and they found that hole and got the cover of it pried halfway up. But just at that moment the farmer who owns this place came to the mill with one of his helpers. The men in the kitchen only just had time to scuttle away, leaving the hole as it was. It was the funniest thing. You'd think it was some new kind of hide-and-seek game. The farmer did some bolting and hammering up—he didn't come inside the kitchen—and then he left.

"Very soon we saw the badger's nose appear at the half-opened stone, trying to get up into the kitchen and scratching away like anything. But soon *he* was disturbed, because the first man—the one who had been living here all the time—appeared again and pulled the stone right up and laid it down as you see it now. But the badger, who had been working underneath, had thrown earth all over the papers, and you couldn't see anything inside but dirt. So the man just left the hole the way it was and set about preparing his supper. And all the time the papers were still lying underneath.

"There the papers would have stayed a while," the bats went on, "if the badger hadn't, late that night when the man was sleeping, again started poking about the hole. He had made up his mind, it seemed, to have that hole for a home, and the first thing he did was to throw the papers out onto the floor of the kitchen. And there the papers lay for anyone to pick up. We supposed," said the bat, "the man who was staying here would find them in the morning and keep them. But the other two fellows came back about an hour after he had gone to sleep. However, he heard them coming and woke up. Then he hid himself and

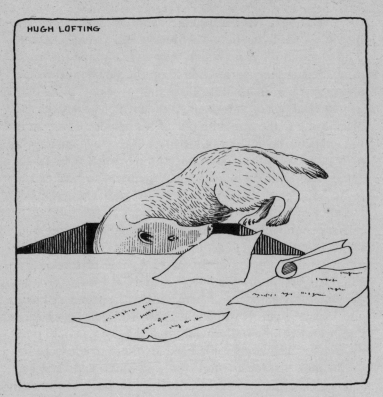

HUGH LOFTING

"The first thing he did was to throw the papers out onto the floor"

watched. The other two did not, of course, know there was anyone staying at the mill.

"And as soon as they felt sure the farmer had gone for the night they entered the kitchen, lit candles, and made themselves at home. And there, the first thing they saw, were the papers they had been looking for, lying on the floor, as large as life. They put them on the table and started going through them. After a while one of them went out to investigate a noise they heard and while he was gone he must have fallen and hurt himself, for he suddenly called to his partner, who left the papers and hurriedly ran out to join him. Then, while they were both gone, the man who was living here sneaked out, took the papers and hid himself again.

"When the two came back they didn't know what to make of it. Finally they decided the mill must be occupied. And, drawing pistols out of their pockets, they went hunting around the place, looking for the man who had taken the papers. But they never found him, and finally, about dawn, when we were thinking of going to bed, they departed in disgust and never showed up again."

"And they left the papers then in the hands of the man who still occupies the mill?" the Doctor asked.

"Yes," said the bats, "so far as we know, he has them still."

"Good heavens!" muttered the Doctor. "What an extraordinary story."

And, turning, he translated what the bats had told him to Steve. Meanwhile the odd creatures went on wheeling in silent circles about the dimly lit room, as though playing a game of tag with their shadows on the walls.

"Splendid!" whispered Steve when the Doctor finished. "Then we may rescue them yet."

John Dolittle turned back to the bats.

"And you never found out where the man hides himself?" he asked.

"Why, certainly," said the bats. "He hides himself in the cellar. He's probably there now."

"But I understood there was no cellar," said the Doctor, gazing down into the hole in the floor. "This gentleman with me lived here for years, and he says he never found one."

"No," said the bats, "no one would find it except by

chance. There's a secret passage to it. The man who lives here blundered on it by accident. It isn't under the part of the floor where the hole is at all. It's under the other half of the kitchen only. Listen, you see that big white stone in the wall over there at about the height of a man's head? Well, you push it at the lower left-hand corner and it will swing inward, showing a passage. Then if you stand on a chair and crawl into the hole you'll find a stairway leading downward on your left, built inside the wall."

Again the Doctor translated to Steve. And the window cleaner got so excited he was all for getting a chair and starting right away. But the Doctor held up his hand.

"We've got to go slowly," he whispered. "We don't know yet whether this man has the papers on him. Wait, now. This needs thinking out."

In whispers, then, the Doctor and Steve worked out a plan of action while the bats went on circling around the guttering candles. Under the table Jip, with ears cocked, sat tense and still, listening for sounds from beneath the floor.

"It is most important," said the Doctor, "not to alarm the man before we are certain where he has those papers. Because once he knows what we're after, you may be sure he'll never let us get a glimpse of them."

"Quite right," whispered Steve. "Certainly he realizes their value. I imagine his idea is to blackmail the agents of the government who came here for them and sell them to them, if he gets a chance. I have no notion who he can be— just some chance shady character, I fancy, who has blundered into this by accident and hopes to make a little money out of it. What plan would you suggest?"

"Let us pretend that we are leaving the mill altogether," said the Doctor. "I don't think he can have any idea yet what we're after. Then we'll come back and watch. If we have luck he may go to the place where he has hidden the papers and give the show away. Then we'll have to rush him and hope to overpower him before he destroys them."

"Your idea is good," said Steve gravely. "Could we overlook the kitchen from the window, do you think?"

"Quite easily," said the Doctor. "But we must be terribly careful that he does not see us or get suspicious. We will begin by noisily making preparations for our departure. When we are outside we can settle other details."

· The Eighth Chapter ·

THE THIEF ESCAPES

THEN suddenly talking out loud, the Doctor closed his bag with a snap. And with much tramping of feet the two of them, followed by Jip, left the mill.

After they had gone about a hundred yards along the path that led down the hill into the town, the Doctor said to Jip, "Now you run on ahead and do a little barking—just like a dog setting out on a walk would do. Don't bother about us; we're going to stay here a while and then go back to the mill. But I want you to continue barking, moving slowly farther away all the time, so the man will think we're going on into the town."

"All right," said Jip. "I understand. But don't forget to whistle for me, if there's a fight."

The Doctor assured Jip that he would. Then, taking Pippinella's small cage out of his pocket, he put the green canary in it and returned it to its hiding place.

"If we should have some trouble," he said to her, "you'll be safer there. Most birds—except bats and owls—don't see too well in the dark."

"Yes," said Pippinella. "That's why we hide ourselves in

the trees when the sun goes down. With cats on the prowl at night that's the only way we can hope to be safe."

"Quite so," said John Dolittle. "Please be very quiet, Pippinella."

By now Jip was off down the hill and Steve and the Doctor could hear him bark out every once in a while, each time a little farther away. After waiting a few minutes they turned and made their way slowly and carefully back.

When they were within about fifty yards of the mill the Doctor motioned to Steve, and they hid themselves behind some bushes.

"I ought to have told those bats to keep me informed," whispered the Doctor. "Silly of me not to have thought of it. Listen! There's somebody opening the kitchen door."

Presently Steve and the Doctor saw the door of the mill open slowly. A man came out and stood motionless, listening. In the distance Jip, still cheerfully yapping for an imaginary man to throw stones, could be plainly heard from below the hill.

After a while the man seemed satisfied that his visitors had really departed for he reentered cautiously and closed the door behind him.

"Look!" said the Doctor. "He's lighting candles. He had hung something over the window, but you can just see a glimmer through the chinks of the door."

The Doctor and Steve were just about to move forward from their hiding place when they heard the faint fluttering of wings near their heads. Against the sky they saw queer little shapes dancing. It was the bats.

"He turned us out," they said to the Doctor. "We wanted to stay and see if we could get you any information. But he flapped us out of the kitchen with a towel. You know some people think we bring bad luck."

"Did you see anything of the papers?" asked the Doctor.

"They hid themselves behind some bushes"

"Yes," said they. "He went and brought them up from the cellar, after he had closed the door and lit the candles. He's examining them on the table. He doesn't seem to be able to read very well because he spends an awful long time over one line. We couldn't find out any more because shortly after he started reading he saw us and drove us out."

"Thank you," said the Doctor, "what you have told us is very valuable." And he translated the bats' information for the benefit of Steve.

"We're going to have a job," the Doctor added, "because that door is probably securely fastened from the inside. And the window is pretty small to get through in a hurry."

"I should think," said Steve, "the best way would be to watch him and wait till he goes out a minute. The chances are that he'll leave them on the table if he does."

"Well," said the Doctor, "let's sneak up and get a look at him, if we can, through the cracks of the door. Then we may be able to know better what to do."

Together, then, the two, taking the utmost care to make no noise, crept forward to the hill till they stood beneath the great towering shadow of the mill. On the left-hand side of the door the woodwork had warped away from the frame, leaving a narrow chink. Through this the Doctor peered.

Inside he saw a ragged, rough-looking man with a stubby growth of beard on his chin, seated at the table. The table was littered deep in papers. Underneath the table was a piece of sacking spread out flat, in which they had evidently been wrapped and carried.

"Tweet! Tweet!" whistled the canary from the Doctor's pocket.

"What is it, Pippinella?" asked John Dolittle, bringing her tiny cage into the open.

"Do you mind if I have a peek at that fellow?" she asked. "I may need to recognize him later."

"Certainly," said the Doctor. And he placed the cage at the opening through which they had been peering.

When she had memorized his features thoroughly the Doctor returned her to his pocket and speaking to Steve said, "If only I knew what kind of a fastening this door had on the inside I could tell what chance we'd have in rushing it. If it gave way to one good heave we might grab the

" 'If I only knew,' he said, 'what kind of a fastening
this door had on the inside' "

fellow and secure your papers before he had time to do
anything."

"No. Better wait," whispered Steve. "If the door should
not break down easily he'd be warned and have lots of
time to destroy the papers in the fireplace or anything else.
Better wait to see if he comes out. Can't you think of a way
to entice him out?"

"Humph!" said the Doctor. "Not without grave risk of

arousing his suspicions and making matters worse than they are. Well, let's wait awhile, then, and see what he does."

So, despite the cold night wind, which had now begun to blow freshly from the east, the Doctor and Steve kept guard at the door, watching through the cracks, hoping the man would get up and come out. John Dolittle had it all planned exactly how they should jump on him, one from each side, and secure him before he had a chance to resist.

But hour after hour went by, and still old Jip kept cheerfully yapping away below the hill and never a sign or a move did the man make.

Finally the Doctor thought he had better go down the hill and relieve poor Jip, who was still performing the part given him and barking cheerily at regular intervals. So, leaving Steve to continue watching, John Dolittle set off down the hill, and finally found Jip—by this time well within the streets of the town—and told him how things were.

"Bother the luck!" muttered Jip. "Well, what are you going to do, Doctor?"

"I don't know, Jip," said John Dolittle. "But we are determined we're going to get those papers, if we have to wait all night."

"How would it be, Doctor," asked the dog, "if I were to moan and whine around the mill? Maybe that would entice him out, and you could jump on him at the door."

"No," said the Doctor, "I think not. We're so afraid of scaring him, you see."

"You couldn't get up on top of the tower and drop down on him from the inside?" asked Jip.

"Not without making enough noise to wake the dead," said the Doctor. "You better stop barking now. You may get the townfolk aroused and do more harm than good. Come on up the hill, nearer the mill, but, for heaven's sake, don't make a sound!"

So once more they proceeded cautiously up the hill, and, after the Doctor had stowed Jip away beneath a hedge and repeated his instructions about keeping quiet, he rejoined Steve at the door.

"Has he moved yet?" he asked.

"Not an inch," whispered the window cleaner. "I believe he's reading my book from beginning to end."

"Tut, tut!" muttered the Doctor. "Luck seems against us tonight. What's that? Oh, the bats again."

Once more the little hovering shadows circled around John Dolittle's head.

"Listen!" the Doctor whispered. "Do you think you could get inside from the top and tell me what kind of a fastening is on this door?"

"Oh, we know already," said the bats. "There is hardly anything at all—just a small, crazy bolt that you could easily force."

"Good," said John Dolittle.

Then he explained to Steve how they were both to draw back and to rush the door together.

"With the weight of the two of us it should surely give," he whispered. "But we must be sure to hit it together. Now, are you ready? Go!"

Together they charged. And together their shoulders hit the panels with a crash. The door gave way to the splintering sound of wood and fell inward. But, unfortunately, the Doctor fell on top of it and tripped Steve up, too. With a sweep of his hand the man at the table put out the candle. The Doctor scrambled to his feet and jumped for where he thought the table was. He found the table, but no man and no papers. The thief had lifted the piece of sacking cloth bodily and rolled it up.

"Guard the door, Steve!" yelled the Doctor. "Don't let him out!"

But he was too late. Steve, overanxious to recover his papers, had already plunged into the dark room and was feeling and stumbling around wildly. Against the patch of sky framed in the doorway the Doctor saw a man's figure, with a bundle under his arm, bound outward into the night.

"Jip!" he yelled. "Jip! Look out, Jip! He's getting away. *And he's got the papers with him!*"

Still calling for Jip, the Doctor jumped over the fallen door and ran out into the open. The wind had now increased and was blowing strongly from the east. John Dolittle, knowing that the man had doubled away to the right, realized at once that the weather was against him. Jip, whom he had left a little below the crest of the hill, was to the windward. Both the Doctor's voice and the man's scent would be carried in the opposite direction.

Thus it was at least two minutes elapsed before John Dolittle could get Jip's attention at all. And by that time the man had got a good start downwind. However, Jip shot away on the trail at once, and the Doctor and Steve blundered after him through the windy night as best they could.

"Even with the weather against him," the doctor panted as he stumbled over the uneven ground, "Jip may yet keep in touch with the scamp. He's a wonder, that dog, when it comes to tracking."

"I only hope that fellow doesn't destroy the papers," muttered Steve.

"No, I don't think that's likely," said John Dolittle. "After all, why should he? He certainly could not make anything out of them if he did that."

"He might want to get rid of evidence that he had stolen them," said Steve.

After about a twenty-minute run, during which the two men entirely lost touch with the dog, they ran into Jip returning from the hunt. His miserable, dejected appearance told them at once that he had met with nothing but failure.

"It's no good, Doctor," said he. "He got away, confound him! As soon as I heard you call I dashed off to try to get ahead of him, where the wind would blow the smell of him toward me, instead of away. But what with the start he had and the crossed trails that wretched old badger had left behind, it couldn't be done. He must have gotten into the woods below the second field—of course, he'd know the country like his own hand, having lived here. And, although my speed is better than his, the lay of the land is new to me. I hunted right through the woods and along every ditch where he might have hidden. The forest was quite large and beyond it I came out on a road. I followed it a way, thinking he'd likely have stuck to it because it gave him a chance for clear running in the dark.

"This road led around, in a wandering sort of zigzag, back into the town on the far side," continued Jip. "There the wind was against me again. And to find him by myself among the houses would be pretty nearly impossible, even if he did not go on through the town—which he probably did. I'm sorry to have failed you, Doctor. But you see how things were, don't you."

"Oh, quite, Jip, quite," said the Doctor. "Too bad, too bad! Have you anything else to suggest that we might do?"

"We could go into the town," said Jip gloomily. "The three of us, by hunting through it thoroughly, *might* run him down. But I have my doubts. I've sort of a notion that

"The three of them made their way down into the town"

customer has been chased before and knows a good deal about the game of lying low."

The Doctor explained to Steve what the dog had said and the three of them, after the door had been put back in its place to keep the rain out, made their way down into the town. By the time they got there it was three o'clock in the morning. As yet, except for a sleepy policeman in the market square, there was no one abroad.

The Doctor had very little hope of accomplishing

anything, but he proceeded with the help of his companions to make a thorough search of all the streets. Each one took a section of the town, and it was agreed that they should meet again in the square after an hour had passed.

But quite early in the hunt John Dolittle realized that it would be perfectly easy for a man to hide, when hunted at such a time as this with all the townsfolk abed, to find some shrubbery in a garden or a stable or other place of refuge, from which he could not be routed without waking up the whole town. And as the nature of their business was something that Steve did not wish to have made public, it would not be possible to arrest him in the ordinary way.

When the Doctor returned to the square the first of the market gardeners were beginning to arrive with their wagons of vegetables. While he waited for the return of Steve and Jip, John Dolittle reviewed the events of the night; he tried to imagine what he would do, were he the hunted man. The only idea that came to him was that he would most likely try to make his way to London, where it would be easy to lose oneself in the crowds. With this in mind he made inquiries of the farmers who were arriving from that direction, hoping to hear that one of them had seen the tramp with the sacking bundle under his arm. But they all gave him the same reply. Nobody had seen the stranger the Doctor described.

Neither Steve nor Jip, when they finally turned up, had any better report to give than his own. It was decided then to have breakfast and talk over what they would do next.

· The Ninth Chapter ·
THE RUNAWAY COACH

REAKFAST was a sad affair. Steve's dejection over the loss of his papers affected all the members of the party. The Doctor sat in silence, eating his boiled egg with little relish, while Steve just pushed the bacon on his plate from one spot to the other.

"You know, John Dolittle," he began, "I don't believe I was ever meant to finish my book. I think I had better drop the whole thing."

"I wouldn't do that," replied the Doctor. "Men like you are needed in this topsy-turvy world. If someone doesn't do something about the unfortunate people in other countries, they may start another war—and then, sooner or later we'd get mixed up in it too. Cheer up, Steve. We're not giving up yet. That fellow may still be lurking around here —waiting for a chance to get a ride up to London."

"And if he does," said Steve, "how on earth are we ever going to find him there?"

"We found you, didn't we?" said the Doctor. "Cheapside and his sparrow gangs spent less than a day doing it too." The Doctor smiled. "I wish we had had him here; that thief wouldn't have gotten very far with your papers."

And turning to Jip, the Doctor went on, "I don't blame you, Jip. Not even a pack of bloodhounds could have held his scent in that wind. But birds—with their ability to dart in and out of trees—could have kept him in sight when he went into the woods."

Jip looked a little crestfallen.

"But, Doctor," he said, "you forget, it was pitch-dark in that woods and—"

"So it was," said the Doctor thoughtfully. "So it was, Jip —I had forgotten. Well, now, don't worry. I still think you're the best tracker I ever knew."

With that Jip brightened up. "The crowds are gathering in the market square," he said. "Couldn't we just walk around and see if I can pick up his scent?"

"A splendid idea, Jip," said John Dolittle. "I'll pay the innkeeper for our breakfast and lodging, and we'll get started."

While explaining the new plan to Steve, the Doctor finished his tea and called for his bill. Pippinella had breakfasted handsomely on toast crumbs and bits of Steve's neglected bacon and was ready to start off on the hunt again. She took her place on her friend's shoulder and said to the Doctor, "Please tell Steve that I can look out for myself. He might waste time trying to protect me when he should be concentrating on catching the rascal who has his papers."

"Yes, indeed, Pippinella," said the Doctor. "I'll explain to him what you said."

Then they walked among the fruit and vegetable stalls, peering into the faces of those who came to buy. Jip kept sniffing at the heels of each passerby until someone accidentally bumped him on the nose with a heavy boot. Jip let out a squeal of pain and rubbed his paw over his aching nose.

"Serves me right," he mumbled. "I'm acting like an

amateur. If he's anywhere around here I'll get his scent without having to put my nose on every pair of heels in the marketplace."

The Doctor and Pippinella laughed at Jip's remark. But Steve, not understanding dog language, looked most put out at the heartlessness of their laughter until the Doctor explained.

"Jip is right," John Dolittle said, after he'd repeated the dog's remark. "We're all too tense. I think we had better go and sit down for a while. We can watch the people coming and going from the bench over there."

The sun was warm and the Doctor and Steve were very tired, not having slept at all the night before. Fully intending to keep a sharp lookout for the thief, they, however, soon found themselves dozing off into a deep slumber. Jip was curled up at the Doctor's feet, his head on his paws, watching, with one eye open and the other snatching a moment of sleep now and then, the people milling about the square. It wasn't long before he, too, gave up and went to sleep.

But Pippinella was wide-awake. Something about the night's adventures had fired her imagination. She felt as if she were living part of her life over again—just which part she couldn't decide. But there was an excitement in the air —a sort of anticipation—as she sat on Steve's sleeping shoulder watching the activity all around her.

Suddenly, as the crowd parted in front of her, Pippinella saw a familiar figure in a cashmere shawl with a market basket on her arm, walk briskly along the path in front of a group of vegetable stalls.

"Aunt Rosie!" whispered Pippinella. "I'd forgotten she lived near here."

Without waking her three companions, the canary flew

over the heads of the villagers and landed on Aunt Rosie's shoulder.

"E-e-e-eh!" squealed the little old lady, dropping her basket and throwing her arms into the air. "What's that? What's that?"

As she turned her head to see what had frightened her she gasped with astonishment.

"Pippinella!" she cried. "I do declare! What a start you gave me. Where did you come from? Why, I thought you were up in London. I saw you in the opera. Quite a celebrity you are these days. And just imagine—you lived in my very own parlor!"

While she chattered on, a gentleman, who had stopped to watch the queer behavior of the little old lady, picked up Aunt Rosie's basket and, with a bow, handed it to her.

"Are you ill, madam?" he asked.

"Certainly not!" she snapped. "I was startled by this bird. She's the prima donna of that famous opera a doctor by the name of Dolittle presented in London a few months ago. You must have read about it in the papers, sir. It made quite a sensation."

"Indeed," said the man, raising his eyebrows quizzically. "But if this is the same bird, what is she doing here? And how is it she picked you to land on?"

"Nincompoop!" muttered Aunt Rosie under her breath. Then, smiling smugly, she answered the stranger.

"Some time ago she used to belong to me. I gave her away to a fellow who washed windows for me. He must have given her to that opera fellow—sold her, most likely; he was very poor. I can't imagine what she is doing here, but she must have recognized me. I wonder if she's lost."

"Perhaps the doctor you speak of is somewhere around here," said the man, glancing over his shoulder. "That might account for the bird's presence."

The idea so surprised Aunt Rosie that she walked abruptly away from the man without so much as a nod. She began peering into the faces of the people around her, searching for the famous impresario of the opera, Doctor Dolittle. Suddenly she stopped.

"Why, my goodness, Pippinella!" she said. "I don't even know what he looks like. Everybody in London was talking about him. And the papers were full of his pictures, but each one was so different from the others I couldn't make up my mind what he *did* look like. I know he wore a high silk hat and—and—"

Aunt Rosie was staring across the square with her head thrust forward. When Pippinella realized that the old lady had spotted the Doctor, she spread her wings and took off for the bench.

"Doctor Dolittle! Wake up!" the canary cried. "Aunt Rosie is coming this way!"

John Dolittle opened his eyes with a start and pushed his hat to the back of his head.

"A—um," he said sleepily. "What did you say, Pippinella?"

"Aunt Rosie is here," Pippinella said. "You remember, Doctor, the little old lady who took me out of the coal mine."

By the time the Doctor had fully awakened and straightened his tie, Aunt Rosie was standing before him. John Dolittle quickly arose and bowed to her.

"Doctor John Dolittle!" she cried. "Why—my gracious me! You're the same man who came to tea that afternoon —and left in such a hurry to catch the coach. Your sister said something about your being a doctor, and all that. But I was so disappointed at your sudden departure, I didn't pay much attention. Imagine me having entertained the great John Dolittle. And didn't know it. I declare! I must tell the ladies of my sewing circle about this."

Doctor Dolittle just stood there—hat in hand. It always confused the modest little man to be treated like a celebrity. He much preferred to allow others to take the bows and receive the praise.

"Good morning, madam," he said, bowing to cover up his shyness. "I'm very happy to see you again."

With that, Aunt Rosie let loose a flood of questions. How had the Doctor come by Pippinella? Did he know his sister, Sarah, had moved to Liverpool? Was he planning any more operas to be presented in London? Did he ever locate that fellow, the window cleaner? Wouldn't he please come to tea some day soon and meet the ladies of the sewing circle?

The Doctor kept opening and closing his mouth in an effort to answer each question as it tumbled forth. But Aunt Rosie didn't give him a chance; she wasn't really concerned with the answers—all she wanted to do was to engage the Doctor's attention long enough so that her friends around the marketplace should see her talking to the famous John Dolittle.

Suddenly, in the middle of another question, she caught sight of Steve, who had awakened and shoved his hat off his face where it had served as a shield against the bright sun. Pointing her finger at him, she cried, "Why, there he is now—the window cleaner! Whatever happened to *you*, my good man? I thought surely you'd be back to do my windows again. That maid of mine, Emily, is simply no good at it. Are you still in the window-washing business?"

While Aunt Rosie was chattering on, Steve had risen from the bench, removed his hat, and was waiting for the flood of questions to cease so that he could answer one of them, at least.

"No, madam," he finally managed to say. "I'm living with the Doctor now. You see, the window washing was just a means to an end—a way to earn some money so that I could get back to London."

"Well, I'm not surprised," said the old lady. "I knew there was something different about you. I suppose you're in one of the arts—as the Doctor is?"

"In a way," Steve replied.

The Doctor, realizing that Aunt Rosie would not stop probing until she discovered something she could take to her sewing-circle friends, decided to bring the interview to an end. He took his gold watch out of his pocket and consulted it.

"We really must be going, Aunt Rosie," he said. "It's ten minutes to eight and we—"

"Oh, my gracious!" interrupted the woman. "The coach for London will be here any moment. I came up to market to get some eggs for my sister—she lives in Knightsbridge, you know. Has six children and uses a tremendous quantity of food. And they get the most abominable eggs in the city—not fit to feed to a pig! It gives me a good excuse to pay her a visit every fortnight or so. Today I'm taking her some cheese as well. Did you ever taste our local cheese, Doctor? It's made right here in Wendlemere. There's none better, I tell you—finer than imported."

"Indeed!" said the Doctor. "I must try it sometime."

He glanced at Steve, who was waiting uncomfortably for Aunt Rosie to stop talking. The window cleaner stepped to the old lady's side and offered her his arm.

"May I escort you to your coach, madam?" he asked politely, knowing that John Dolittle was having a difficult time getting rid of Aunt Rosie.

"I must get my eggs and cheese first," she said, taking his

arm. "We can chat on the way. Good-bye, Doctor. Don't forget your promise to come to tea one day."

John Dolittle nodded as they hurried away. Pippinella, who had been on Steve's shoulder all during the conversation, called out as they left the Doctor and Jip.

"I'll just go along with Steve, if you don't mind, Doctor. I may catch a glimpse of that fellow in the crowd. If I do, I'll be back in a hurry."

The Doctor and Jip watched Steve piloting Aunt Rosie among the stalls as she made her purchases. Finally they saw them heading toward the coach stop at the north end of the square. In the distance could be heard the clippity-clop of horses' hooves and the jingle of harness as the London coach approached the town. Over the various sounds that accompanied a market gathering the Doctor heard the clear, sweet voice of the canary as she gayly sang the harness jingle song.

"Pippinella is happy again with her master," he said to Jip. "I suppose the jingle of the harness recalls the song she composed when she lived at the Inn of the Seven Seas."

"Yes," said Jip. "It's good to hear her singing again. I hope nothing happens to part her from her friend—now that he's found."

As they listened, the sound of the approaching coach grew louder. In the distance, the Doctor could see Aunt Rosie with her arm upraised as a signal to the driver to stop. Business around the marketplace momentarily suspended while merchants and townspeople turned their heads to watch the coach from the north arrive.

Suddenly, with a thundering of hoofs and a rumble of carriage wheels, the coach tore past the stop and continued right on through the marketplace. People scattered in fright; chickens and ducks ran for their lives, their feathers flying; and the dust threw a screen over the whole town.

"What do you make of that?" asked Jip, looking puzzled. "The driver certainly could see that Aunt Rosie wanted to get on."

"It's very odd," said the Doctor. "Wendlemere is a regular stop on this coach route. It didn't look as though the horses were running away, either. Oh, look, Jip! Here comes Pippinella."

The green canary landed with a fluttering of wings on the Doctor's outstretched hand. Her eyes were watering from the dust cloud through which she'd flown. She was gasping for breath.

"Dear me!" exclaimed the Doctor. "You might have crashed into a tree—flying blind like that. Now, rest a moment before you try to talk."

He held her gently in his hand until she could speak.

"You saw what happened, Doctor?" she finally managed to gasp between breaths.

"Yes," replied John Dolittle. "And it was most puzzling. Didn't the driver see Aunt Rosie?"

"He saw her, all right!" answered the canary. "But he drove by, anyway. There's something strange about it. I know that man. He's the most reliable driver on this road."

"What do you mean, Pippinella?" said the Doctor. "Did you say you recognized the coachman?"

"Yes, Doctor," replied the canary. "I saw his face very clearly. He's my old friend, Jack—the one who used to bring me a lump of sugar when he stopped at the Inn of the Seven Seas."

"Then something surely is amiss!" said the Doctor. "Pippinella, could you catch up to that coach?"

"Certainly!" she said. "I can outfly him by fifty times his speed."

"Well, go quickly, then!" said the Doctor, raising his hand so that she could take off. "And find out why he didn't stop. I'll be busy here getting help, should we need it. Report back to me as soon as you can."

· The Tenth Chapter ·
THE PAPERS RECOVERED—
AND PUDDLEBY AGAIN

WHEN the green canary left the Doctor's hand she darted through the leafy oaks that circled the market square. As she reached the outskirts of town she could see, in the distance, a cloud of dust that marked the swiftly disappearing coach. Cutting across a field to where the road swerved to the right, she overtook the galloping horses and lit on the driver's shoulder.

"Jingle! Jingle! Crack and tingle. Coachman hold your horses!" she sang at the top of her lungs so as to be heard above the racket of the rumbling wheels. This song, she felt sure, Jack would remember, as she had sung it to him every time his coach had entered the courtyard of the Inn of the Seven Seas.

"Pippinella!" he cried. "My old friend, Pippinella."

But instead of smiling at her he drew his brows together and, grasping the reins more tightly in his hands, urged the panting horses on.

"Go away, Pip!" he yelled. "Go away! There's danger here!"

But Pippinella clung more tightly than ever to the cloth of Jack's coat. Sensing that something was seriously wrong, she dug her claws more firmly into the fabric and leaned way out to see who rode in the body of the carriage. A face with a stubbly beard and piercing black eyes hung out of the window. In his hand the man held a big black pistol that he was aiming at Jack's head.

It was the thief who had stolen the window cleaner's papers!

"Go away, I say!" shouted Jack again. "You'll get hurt if that rascal decides to pull the trigger!"

An evil gleam came into the eyes of the thief. He brandished the pistol. "Who are y' callin' a rascal?" he screamed. "I'll blow yer into kingdom come if yer gets sassy with me!"

Pippinella flew to Jack's other shoulder so as not to further antagonize the dangerous passenger. For a moment or two she wondered what she had better do. Then, remembering the Doctor's orders to report back to him as soon as she could, the canary flew into the air and headed back to town.

Meanwhile the Doctor had not been idle. With the help of Jip he had rounded up a half-dozen mongrel dogs who were noted for their bravery and fighting ability.

"Listen," said the Doctor in dog language when they had ceased barking their pleasure at meeting the famous animal physician. "Can I count on you for some help—if I need it?"

"Why, sur-r-re, sur-r-re!" said Mac, a Scottish terrier of mixed origin. "We're verra happy to assist ye, Doctor Dolittle. What is it ye want done?"

"I don't know yet," replied the Doctor. "But it may be very dangerous." And glancing from one to the other of the eager faces watching him, he went on, "Are you all agreed on Mac's decision?"

The dogs answered the Doctor with a perfect avalanche of tail-waggings, ear-scratchings, and nose-twitchings.

"Come with me, then!" ordered John Dolittle. And he started down the London road at a fast clip with Steve at his side and Jip and the pack of mongrel dogs at his heels.

As he scanned the sky for some sight of Pippinella, the Doctor heard the thud of a small object on his high silk hat. Reaching up to investigate, he felt the clutching on his finger of a pair of tiny claws.

"It's you, Pippinella," he said, lowering his hand as he continued running.

"No, it ain't 'you, Pip,' " said the bird. "It's me, Cheapside! And I'd like t'know where *yer* goin'—and in such a 'urry. It ain't good for your 'eart, Doc."

"Never mind that now," said the Doctor. "I'm delighted to see you again, Cheapside. How does it happen you are down this way?"

"I didn't 'appen—as you say, Doc," said the London sparrow. "I were lookin' for you. Becky went off to visit 'er maw, who's buildin' a new 'ome in Hyde Park—uppitty, the old girl's gotten since she landed on the Queen's bonnet during a parade last week. Says Piccadilly ain't no fit place for a bird what's sat on the Queen's new 'at. Well, as I was sayin', Becky went off for the day, and I thought I'd 'ave a run down to Puddleby to see 'ow you was gettin' on. When I found you wasn't there I 'ad a quick look 'round—Lor' bless me, Doc, things is in a mess. Then I went to Greenheath and 'eard 'ow you was off on another 'unt—for some missin' papers. Say, Doc, slow up a bit, will you? I 'ave to shout me lungs out to make myself 'eard. And what's the 'ounds doin' at yer 'eels? Say the word, and I'll peck out their eyes!"

"No, no, Cheapside!" cried the Doctor. "We're on our way to help Pippinella's friend, Jack, the coachman."

As the Doctor was about to continue, he saw a tiny speck in the sky coming closer and closer.

"Here comes Pippinella now!" he said, slowing to a walk. "She'll tell you the rest."

The little party stood in the road and waited for the canary to arrive.

"She flies good—for a primer donner—don't she?" said the sparrow.

When the little canary landed on the Doctor's hand she had to sit gasping for a moment before she could speak. Then she described the predicament Jack was in.

"And the man with the pistol," gasped Pippinella, "is *the fellow who stole Steve's papers!*"

"Are you sure?" asked the Doctor.

"Absolutely!" replied the canary. "One never forgets a face as ugly as his."

"What about Steve's papers?" John Dolittle asked anxiously. "Did he have them with him?"

"I don't know," replied Pippinella. "But in any case we must help Jack."

"Yes, indeed!" said the Doctor. "We must carry out our plan quickly now," he continued. He translated the canary's story to Steve in as few words as possible. Then turning to Jip, he said, "Jip, take Mac and the others and follow Pippinella as fast as you can. Catch up to that coach and tell the horses I want them to stop. Mac, while Jip is explaining to the horses, you get into that carriage and see that that rascal doesn't use his pistol!"

"We're on our way!" cried Jip. "That thief isn't going to get away this time!"

"Wait for me," cried Cheapside. "What makes you think I ain't goin' along to 'ave some fun too?"

The two birds shot into the air as the pack of dogs led by Jip raced down the road. By now the coach was no more than a tiny speck on the horizon, and it took the strange group of pursuers a good ten minutes of their best speed to close the ever-increasing distance between them. When they began to near the speeding carriage the dust became so thick they could barely see one another, nor could they breathe with comfort.

"Cut across this hayfield!" called Pippinella from above. "The road makes a sharp turn just before those elms. We can reach the place ahead of the coach and cut them off."

With Pippinella and Cheapside flying low over the standing grain, the dogs followed through the hay, leaving a path behind them like the wake of a ship at sea. When they broke into the open the canary was ahead of them, pointing the way with her bill.

"That's the spot—over there!" she cried. "Follow me!"

They reached the shelter of the big elms as the coach rounded the bend. It was lurching from side to side as the horses pounded on in panic. Jack continued to urge them on while the man in the back hung out of the window shouting orders and waving his pistol in the air.

Jip dashed into the road and raced beside the galloping horses.

"Stop!" he cried. "Doctor Dolittle orders you to stop!"

"We can't," whined the horse on Jip's side. "If we do, Jack will be killed!"

"Do what I tell you!" Jip commanded, nipping at the horse's foreleg. "The other dogs will take care of that fellow with the pistol!"

Cheapside, sitting on the horse's ear, leaned over and shouted into it, "Do like he tells you, Milly! Else I'll peck out yer eyes!"

"Oh, hello, Cheapside," said Milly. "I'm happy to see you again."

"Never mind the pink-tea chatter, you dumb wagon-puller!" screamed the sparrow. "The Doc says stop! And I'm 'ere to see 'is horders is carried out!"

Milly turned her head nervously and looked back over her shoulder while she raced on. She saw that what Jip had said was true: the dogs, led by Mac, the Scottish terrier, were jumping and clawing their way through the open window of the speeding carriage. The thief had disappeared from the window, and the sound of scuffling could be heard from within. The exhausted mare turned to her teammate and, puffing and panting, said, "Stop, Josephine! It's all right. Those dogs have taken care of that fellow. Thank goodness, Jack is safe and we can stop this senseless running."

Gradually the two mares brought the lumbering coach to a halt. With relief from the nervous strain they became quite hysterical and wept openly.

"Brace up, me 'earties!" said Cheapside. "There ain't no cause fer weepin'. You only did what you 'ad to!"

Milly shook the tears from her eyes and nudged Josephine with her nose.

"Cheapside's right," she said. "It wasn't our fault."

With the stopping of the coach, the thief managed to turn the handle on the door, and man and dogs tumbled out into the dusty road. He tried to get onto his feet to make a break for freedom, but the dogs piled onto him and bore him to the ground again. Pippinella and Cheapside kept making short dives at his head, pecking him on the ears and generally worrying him into complete confusion.

" 'Elp! 'elp!" yelled the frightened man. "Call off your dogs! I'll come quiet-like!"

Jack, with carriage whip in hand, stood over the milling mass of dogs and man.

"You're not so brave now," he said, "without your pistol."

Jip, seeing that Mac and his gang had the situation well

in hand, was hunting frantically for the bundle of missing papers. With a yelp of joy he found them under the seat of the coach where the thief had hoped to conceal them.

"Pip! Pip!" he yelled. "Come here! I've found Steve's papers!"

Meanwhile, down the winding road could be seen the rapidly approaching figures of the Doctor and Steve, their jackets billowing out behind them. Pippinella flew to meet them with the good news that the papers had been recovered. The Doctor told Steve what Pippinella had said.

"Good old Pip!" said Steve. "You're the best friend a man ever had."

"Oh, I didn't do anything," replied the canary. "Jip was the one. He's guarding them until you get there."

Again the Doctor interpreted.

When they reached the coach they found Jack trying to persuade Jip to let him have the bundle of papers. Knowing nothing of their history, he naturally supposed they belonged to the man the dogs were holding and that they would disclose his identity.

"Good doggy," Jack was saying as he poked his head into the carriage and tried to remove the bundle. "I won't harm them."

But Jip was adamant. He didn't know Jack—except through Pippinella—and he wasn't going to take any chances. He growled and bared his teeth at the coachman. But when he saw the Doctor framed in the open carriage doorway he let out a yelp of welcome.

"Thank goodness, you've come!" he said. "I didn't want to have to bite Pip's friend. But I was determined to do it if he insisted on removing Steve's papers."

The Doctor took the bundle and handed it to Steve.

"Excellent work!" he said to Jip. "I'm proud of you.

"The dogs all piled helter-skelter on top of the cringing man"

Come—we'll take a look at this rascal who has given us so much trouble." John Dolittle—with a smile at the comical positions of the dogs all piled helter-skelter on top of the cringing man—said to Mac, "You may release him now. I want a word with him."

The dogs untangled themselves, shook their rumpled coats, and came to stand beside the Doctor. As the man got to his feet the Doctor turned again to Mac.

"You and your friends are excellent hunters," he said.

"Not a scratch on your quarry. I want to commend you very highly."

"Thank you, Doctor Dolittle," said the Scottish terrier. "It was a bit difficult—when he got rambunctious—not t'nip his ears. But we remembered what ye said t'us aboot not drawin' blood."

The man, puzzled by the strange maneuvers of the Doctor and Mac—for, of course, they spoke in dog language—turned his head frantically from left to right, looking for a means of escape.

"I wouldn't make any attempts to get away if I were you," said the Doctor. "My friends here would overtake you in the matter of moments. And I'm not so sure I'd caution them against tearing you to pieces this time."

"I didn't mean no 'arm, governor!" whined the man. "I were just lookin' for a place t' get out of the weather when I seen those fellows a'sneakin' around the old mill and a'diggin' under the floor. 'Well,' I says to myself, 'there must be something mighty important in this 'ere mill. I'll stick around and see what it is.'"

By this time everyone—Steve, Jack, Pippinella, and Cheapside—had joined the Doctor and the pack of dogs and were listening to the stranger's story.

"Like I said," continued the man. "I ain't no regular thief. I thought if those papers were so important to somebody else, they might fetch a bob or two if I could find the right person. They weren't no good to me, goodness knows, I couldn't make 'ead nor tail of 'em. All full of political talk—and about foreigners, at that. Please, governor, let me go. I ain't done no 'arm. If I'd 'a' knowed this bloke were the rightful owner, I'd 'a' been 'appy to turn them over to 'im."

Steve and the Doctor exchanged a glance, and the window cleaner, smiling, nodded.

"All right," said the Doctor to the relief of all the party, who were feeling sorry for the man and didn't want to see him punished, after all. "You may go. But try and stay out of trouble from now on. The police might not be so lenient with you."

While the man started back up the road toward Wendlemere, the Doctor thanked Mac and his friends for their assistance and dismissed them with a promise to return some day and pay them a visit.

Cheapside, perched on top of the coach, spoke to the Doctor. "Is it 'ome to Puddleby now, Doc?" he asked.

"Yes, Cheapside," replied the Doctor. "It's home to Puddleby at last! I'm ready for a good long rest by the fireside."

"Ho, ho!" laughed the sparrow. "If it's rest you want, Doc, better not go 'ome. The 'ouse looks like a bloomin' 'ospital, it does—since some gossipin' bluejays passed the word 'round that you might be comin' back. Chipmunks with busted paws sleepin' all over the place, 'orses with 'eaves lodgin' two to a stall in the stable, and a sneakin' weasel with her 'ole brood a' nasty little brats coughin' their 'eads off under the 'ouse."

"Oh, dear," sighed the Doctor. "Then I must get there quickly. I'd feel terrible if one of them should die because it hadn't had the proper care."

Jack insisted on driving the whole party home to Puddleby.

"Oh, I couldn't let you do that," said John Dolittle. "You see, we must go to Greenheath first and collect the rest of my family."

"Well, that's all right," the coachman said. "Greenheath is on the way to Puddleby."

"But there must be other passengers on the road waiting for you at this very moment," said the Doctor.

"Probably," said Jack. "But I'm so late now it doesn't

matter. The twelve o'clock coach will be along shortly and can pick up anyone bound for London. Besides," Jack continued, "you saved my life and I'd like to show my gratitude in some small way. Hop in, and we'll get started."

"Well," said the Doctor, hesitating. "If you're sure it will be all right we'd be delighted to go home in such splendor. My, my! Our own private coach! Won't Gub-Gub be surprised. Come along, Steve and Pippinella."

"We don't want to be a bother, Doctor," said the window cleaner. "Pip and I can go up to London and—"

"Nonsense!" declared the Doctor. "There's plenty of room at Puddleby. You can finish your book and enjoy some of Dab-Dab's excellent cooking at the same time. There is nothing she likes better than to have a company of hungry people around her table. Now, now," he continued as Steve began to protest further, "I won't hear of anything else. Get aboard everybody. We're off for Greenheath and home—home to Puddleby at last!"

The End

· About the Author ·

HUGH LOFTING was born in Maidenhead, England, in 1886 and was educated at home with his brothers and sister until he was eight. He studied engineering in London and at the Massachusetts Institute of Technology. After his marriage in 1912 he settled in the United States.

During World War One he left his job as a civil engineer, was commissioned a lieutenant in the Irish Guards, and found that writing illustrated letters to his children eased the strain of war. "There seemed to be very little to write to youngsters from the front; the news was either too horrible or too dull. One thing that kept forcing itself more and more upon my attention was the very considerable part the animals were playing in the war. That was the beginning of an idea: an eccentric country physician with a bent for natural history and a great love of pets. . . ."

These letters became *The Story of Doctor Dolittle*, published in 1920. Children all over the world have read this book and the eleven that followed, for they have been translated into almost every language. *The Voyages of Doctor Dolittle* won the Newberry Medal in 1923. Drawing from the twelve *Doctor Dolittle* volumes, Hugh Lofting's sister-in-law, Olga Fricker, later compiled *Doctor Dolittle: A Treasury*, which was published by Dell in 1986 as a Yearling Classic.

Hugh Lofting died in 1947 at his home in Topanga, California.